# A Southern Lights Christmas

By

USA Today Bestselling Author

## Lauren Gayle

Southern Lights: Book 1

I0517506

Copyright © 2020 Cajunflair Publishing

ISBN: 978-1-940305-46-2

This story is a work of fiction. Names, characters, places and incidents are either products of the author's imagination or, in the case of real cities, clubs, theaters or restaurants mentioned in the story, are used in a fictitious manner. Any resemblance to actual events, or persons, living or dead, is entirely coincidental.

All rights reserved.

No part of this publication can be reproduced or transmitted in any form or by any means, electronic or mechanical, without permission in writing from the author.

*Chapter 1*

Natalie pulled the fully extended handle of her carryon bag, longed to be anywhere else in the world but here.

She followed her parents to a row of empty seats at the far side of the Louis Armstrong airport waiting area. Scanning the area, she figured her mom would change seats three times before settling into that ever elusive just-the-right-spot. All airport chairs were alike, for crying out loud, each one as generically uncomfortable as the next. Nat parked her bag at one end of a row with a tarmac view. Her mom moved a third time—*nailed it*—finding her sweet spot directly across the aisle from Natalie.

Within seconds of positioning their various items of luggage and other accessories, her father wrapped one arm around her mother's shoulders in his usual show of touchy-feely affection. Her mom clasped her husband's free hand and lifted her face to him. He planted a kiss on her mouth with a loud smack.

Natalie squeezed her eyelids shut, super-annoyed by their all too normal overload of sweetness. Before this vacation ended, she'd need insulin injections.

She opened her eyes but averted her gaze. Nothing actually wrong with high school sweethearts still being in love after thirty-six years of marriage. That's how it should be, right? Sweet mother of Jesus, did they *have* to be so—visual and vocal about it?

Nat suffered in silence through five more minutes of her dad's affectionate pecks to his wife's cheek, prompting school-girlish giggles from her mom. She stood suddenly, draping her purse strap over one shoulder. "I want to stretch my legs for a bit. Maybe find some coffee. You lovebirds want anything?"

Too engrossed in each other to hear their daughter's question, neither Nan or Neil DeVille responded. Nat emitted a low snort of disgust and hurried away, hoping to head off her gag reflex.

To be fair, she hadn't minded her parent's sappy shows of affection at all up until a year ago. For as long as she could remember, everyone in her circle of friends had wished for parents like hers. Too many of her peers had grown up in divided homes with single parents or step-parents and siblings—situations in which most resulted in one form of drama or another. All had required major adjustments for everyone involved.

In stark contrast, Nat's homelife had been a wonderful and stable environment for her. As a result, she had expected nothing less from her own marriage. She'd met Craig Bradford at twenty, married him at twenty-two, and for the most part, their eight years of marriage had been just as stable and loving as her parent's.

Until it hadn't.

Natalie settled for a bottle of water and walked slowly, sipping from it. She leaned against a wall and stared out at one section of the runway, watching an incoming plane taxi in with its load of passengers. Her phone vibrated and she glanced at the message from Pam, her best friend since sixth grade.

*If you have time to talk please call me.*

Natalie frowned. A preferred texter, Pam, or PJ to her best friend, never asked to talk unless there was trouble. She hit the phone icon and her friend picked up on the first ring. "What's wrong, PJ?"

"I just called off my engagement, Nat."

"Oh no! What happened?"

"I c-c-aught Dustin with his co-worker and—it wasn't pretty."

Natalie closed her eyes, willing a better outcome for her bestie. "Any hope of a silly misunderstanding that could be explained away after a little space and cooler heads?" Pam's sigh carried through the phone and Nat pictured her friend placing one hand over her eyes as she prepared to answer.

"I'd told you his company was opening a new location in their Southwest Louisiana branch, right?"

Natalie switched her phone to her other hand. "Yeah, in Lake Charles or Sulphur, right?"

"It's in Lake Charles; he's been spending a lot of time there. So, I booked the entire week of Christmas through New Year's Day at this ... Mistletoe Lodge ... just north of Lake Charles. It's a rustic looking, log cabin lodge—a bed and breakfast type set-up—in the middle of the woods. Quaint, but pretty from what I see of the photos. It has great reviews. I wanted to spend some time with him in a relaxed atmosphere, you know?"

"I can understand that." Nat kept her response short, hoping to hear the story before her plane boarded.

"I went to his apartment early to prepare a home cooked meal for him and surprise him with the reservations. He'd given me a key to his apartment the last time I spent the day there so I used it to get inside. I only had time to dump the groceries on the kitchen table and run to the bathroom. When I was still in there, I heard someone come into the apartment. I finished and stepped out quietly, still hoping to surprise him. I tiptoed into the living room and there they were, half-undressed on the couch and—you guess the rest."

"I'm so sorry, PJ. I truly am." Natalie had never thought much of Dustin but had kept her doubts to herself. She'd prayed that her instincts were wrong about the guy who'd swept Pam up into a whirlwind relationship, followed with a too-soon-for-comfort engagement. Unfortunately, Nat's instincts had been on point.

"I figure *she's* the reason he spent so much time in Lake Charles instead of coming home on weekends."

Nat didn't dare voice her agreement. "I'm so sorry you had to see that." *But better now than after the 'I do's'.*

"Now I'm stuck with this week-long reservation at the Southern Lights Mistletoe Lodge. Non-refundable, at this point, I'm sure."

"Have you called to ask?"

"No. I guess it wouldn't hurt to try though. It looks like such a beautiful little place. I was so looking forward to this."

"You could go anyway." Maybe she'd meet someone there who'd make her forget all about stupid Dustin. This too, Nat kept to herself.

"I just couldn't, Nat. Being there, without him. It'd be too much to bear."

"I'm so sorry, PJ. You didn't deserve that."

"Well—" Pam went through a series of sniffles on her end of the phone. "As bad as it is to lose someone through cheating, it's nothing compared to someone dy—" She cut her sentence short. "I'm sorry, Nat."

"Death is death, PJ. Death of a husband or death of a relationship. Don't minimize your pain just because Dustin the cheater is still alive." She saw her parents rise from their seats and look around for her. "Oh, sweet Lord," she groaned. "I think it's time to board."

"Have a good trip, Nat. The weather should be fabulous in the Bahamas."

"Honestly, I'd rather be going anywhere else rather than to the Bahamas with my parents."

"Why did you agree to it?"

"Because my mother was on a one-woman crusade to make sure I didn't spend Christmas at home alone. You know how she is—she doesn't acknowledge the word 'no'." She groaned again as her mom spotted her and waved. "They've seen me, darn it. I've pussy-footed around and missed my window of opportunity to escape."

"Too bad you can't take my reservation."

"I know. A secluded lodge in the woods sounds pretty good to me right now."

"But then, why couldn't you?"

Natalie stood stock still, all previous notions of Bahamas coming to a grinding halt. "Why couldn't I?"

"That's what I said."

In less than ten seconds, Nat had solidified her decision. "Text me all the info, Pam. If it's paid in advance, I'll reimburse you. I love you, hon. Got to go now but I'll call you once I've rented a car and I'm on the road." Natalie ended the call, grabbed her carryon handle and met her parents halfway. "Mom…dad…I love you both and I'm sure you'll have a fabulous time in the Bahamas. But something came up and I won't be going with you."

"What? But we're about to board!" Nan's eyes widened. "You can't just leave!" she sputtered while pulling at her short blond hair, a surefire sign of her being rattled.

Natalie smiled. "Sure, I can. People miss flights all the time. Honest, mom…I appreciate the effort you put into planning this but going to the Bahamas as a third wheel in the greatest love story of all time is not my idea of a good time." She hugged them both and left with one last "Love you guys!" called over her shoulder before heading for the nearest car rental desk.

# Chapter 2

December 20th

"Would you look at all that beautiful green?" Mack stared at the Louisiana landscape below from the plane's window seat.

"Pardon?"

He turned toward the woman seated beside him. "I'm from northern Minnesota, ma'am and I've been shoveling myself out of my front door for nearly two months. I'm amazed anytime I see green grass in the middle of winter."

The woman smiled, her eyes glazing over as though she were recalling the past. "I grew up in Wisconsin, dear. I understand completely. I taught school and hired someone to do the shoveling, but getting to and from work on icy roads wore me out." She leaned over and spoke in a conspiratorial whisper. "I moved south years ago—no regrets." She winked. "It's something to think about."

Mack unbuckled his seat belt as the plane rolled to a dead stop, anxious to feel the warmth of sunshine on his bare skin. "I hear you, ma'am."

* * *

With his heavy overcoat slung over one arm, Mack hefted his duffle and approached a silver-haired man of medium build and his own height of six feet tall, give or take an inch. The man held a sign that read SOUTHERN LIGHTS MISTLETOE LODGE in bold letters. "Are you my welcome wagon?"

The gentleman cocked his head. "Your name, please?"

Mack stopped in front of him, his hand extended. "I'm Mack Henry."

The other man grinned and shook his hand, his grip strong, obviously accustomed to hard work. "I'm here for *you*. Drew Brunson, co-owner and proprietor of Southern Lights Mistletoe Lodge." He winked. "Sorry about that, but a fellow can't be too careful these days." He reached for Mack's duffle. "Is that it?"

Mack waved off his offer and hefted the bag to his shoulder. "Thanks Mr. Brunson, but I've got it."

"Mr. Brunson was my dad and grandad. Call me Drew."

"Sure, if you promise to call me Mack."

They approached a forest green van boasting the lodge logo on its sliding door. "How far is it to this lodge?'

"A good forty-minute drive northeast from here. We're not too far from the Lake Charles metropolis, but secluded enough to be surrounded by nature and all its glory."

They loaded up and Mack settled into the front passenger seat beside Drew. Within minutes they were driving into south Lake Charles. The older man pulled to a stop at a bustling intersection, grumbled some about afternoon traffic before turning his attention to Mack. "What do you do for a living, son?"

"I'm the project engineer for a structural engineering company."

Drew faced him. "No kidding? We have a little in common. I was in road construction for forty years." He veered right on the next street. "This is probably your slow season due to winter weather conditions."

"It is." Mack noted they'd headed north again on a roadway marked Louisiana Highway 14. They crossed the Interstate roadway and drove over a bridge labeled English Bayou, reaching a second longer bridge over a river whose name, Calcasieu, mystified him. "How the heck do you pronounce the name of this river—Cal-cas-ee-oo?"

Drew chuckled. "Nice effort but it's pronounced Cal-kuh-shoo, accent on the first syllable. It's named for an Atakapa Indian chief and means 'crying eagle'—apparently his battle cry sounded like an eagle. The whole of Calcasieu Parish is steeped in history. After France ceded Louisiana to the American government, Spain disputed it and this entire area all the way up to the Red River in Alexandria was called the 'neutral strip'—rampant with outlaws and filibusters from several different states. This area has a rich ethnic mixture of Indians, Spanish, Creoles, Acadians and Anglo-Americans."

Mack nodded, always fascinated by the history of a new place. "Where does the name Brunson fit into that mix?"

"Me?" Drew slapped his hand on his thigh and belted out a hardy laugh. "My parents were transplants from Texas. My dad moved us here to work in the oil refineries when I was a kid. I love it here, though."

They drove on, continuing north through Moss Bluff, a bustling little suburb north of Lake Charles. "If you don't mind me asking, how'd you come up with your lodge's name? Mistletoe suggests Christmas—and what kind of southern lights do you have around here?"

"My wife always claimed the night time view from our backyard rivaled the Aurora Borealis. She started calling it our own southern light show. We've been trying to control the mistletoe growing wild in oaks on the property for thirty years. Our kids heard me fuss about it so much they started calling it the Mistletoe Lodge when they were young." He met Mack's gaze, his eyes sparkling with humor. "When we get there, you can see for yourself."

Twenty more minutes of small talk had them turning onto a paved road headed into a dense woody area. Mack sighed at the abundance of green.

"You beginning to regret the location? I know it looks like we're surrounded by woods but we're really not all that isolated."

The space reverberated with Mack's low chuckle. "I'm amazed at all this green in the middle of winter."

"Technically, we're just starting winter—first day today. Heck, we ran the AC last week it got so humid."

Mack grunted. "We've been feeling winter for a few months already. When I left home there wasn't a spot of green to be seen, not even from the plane. I couldn't stand the thought of another Christmas with a snow blower for company." He looked at Drew. "I needed a break." Curious about their destination, Mack continued his line of questioning. "This lodge of yours—was it built specifically to be a bed and breakfast?"

Mack grinned. "No, it started as a summer and winter getaway cabin when our kids were young. What realtors today describe as a 'rustic fixer upper'. We expanded over the years, even added a second story.

Once our three kids left the nest, we sold the place to a couple who turned it into a bed and breakfast. It broke our hearts to get rid of it, so I asked them if they ever decided to sell to give us first choice. Five years later, when the wife and I both retired from our full-time jobs we bought it back from them." He turned onto a gravel road, splayed his fingers on the steering wheel. "We sold our house, gave the lodge a facelift and some upgrades and turned it into a thriving business for the last ten years. It's been good to us, but I'm ready for a change."

"A new business venture?"

"Heck no! I've about convinced the wife it's time to do some traveling. I'm seventy years old and still haven't seen the Grand Canyon, Niagara Falls, or Mount Rushmore. I plan to do that before I die."

"You don't look like you're ready for the bone-yaahd." Mack put a New England spin on the word, drawing a round of hearty laughter from Drew.

"Not yet, but our friends are starting to drop like flies hit with shots of bug spray. I don't want to take any chances."

Mack couldn't argue with that, so he kept quiet until they pulled into a clearing on a few acres of open land. He whistled in appreciation at the large, two-storied log cabin flanked on one side by a towering oak. The van stopped in front of wooden steps connected to a deep porch, railed on both sides and spanning the entire width of the house. It held several heavy wooden rockers, large potted poinsettias and Norfolk pines, all glittering with tiny, clear lights. Bright red bows hyphenated lengths of green garland, creating a warm festive appearance. A large yellow dog rose from the porch deck and barked a greeting, its fluffy tail fanning the air with exuberant waves.

"That's old Duke. He used to be my hunting buddy before we both grew too old and full of aches."

"Golden Retriever?"

"Yep."

"Are you partial to that breed for hunting?"

"Not really." Drew grinned at him. "Just partial to Duke, in particular, I guess." They exited the van and Drew leaned over to ruffle the dog's fur. "How you doing today, old man?"

Mack lowered to one knee, extended his hand to the large dog whose muzzle shined with silver. "Hey boy, you're getting up there in age, aren't you?" The dog warmed to him instantly, its huge fluffy tail wagging in appreciation at Mack's attention.

"He's twelve years old and if that bunk about dog years is true, he's got me beat by fourteen years already." Drew pointed to the huge towering oak next to the lodge. "You see the clusters of mistletoe in that tree?" He continued at Mack's nod. "The darn parasite loves that old oak and others on the property. But our trees are hearty, so the damage is minimal."

Mack grabbed his bag and followed Drew inside. He studied the lodge's typical but pristine log cabin style interior, decorated to the hilt for the Christmas season. A huge, but inviting living area filled with a mixture of overstuffed cloth and leather furniture circled the room's focal point, a massive stone fireplace. Every single detail in the room screamed *Welcome, relax, and enjoy your time with us*. He walked over to a huge Christmas tree decorated beautifully with elements found in nature, and interspersed with small wooden duck decoys. He examined one closely, flipped it over to see D.B. on the bottom. "Is carving a hobby of yours, Drew?"

Drew appeared at his side. "My grandpa used to carve his own wooden duck decoys back in the day. My dad picked it up from him and I did the same. Beth asked me years ago to make some miniatures for the tree. I've carved no less than four or five a year for the last twenty years."

Mack examined a few more before turning back to Drew. "A buddy of mine makes a killing from online sales for his hand carved items. This hobby of yours could turn into a lucrative little business."

Drew shrugged off the suggestion. "If I did it for profit it'd take all the fun out of it. It'd feel more like a job than a hobby, you know?"

"Well, hello! You must be our new guest."

Mack turned towards the female greeting, approving of the way Drew placed his arm around the woman and gave her peck on the cheek. She blushed ever so slightly at his attentions; her sparkling blue eyes set off by a halo of snow-white hair. The pretty woman and Drew seemed made for each other.

"I guess I am, ma'am. I'm Mack Henry." He reached for her extended hand and shook it gently.

"I recognize the voice from our phone conversation when you booked. You're here to escape the frigid Minnesota winter," she finished for him. "I'm Beth Brunson, Mack, and welcome to Southern Lights Mistletoe Lodge. Our goal is to make sure your stay is as pleasant and relaxing as possible." She leaned forward to whisper. "So, you'll keep coming back for years to come." She took his arm and led him to a desk area against the opposite wall. "Come on over here and let's get you all signed in and comfortable. I've given you the Fleur de Lis suite, pending your approval, of course. I'll ask you to fill out a card with your breakfast preferences every evening so we can be sure to have them included on the buffet in the mornings from 7:00 to 9:30."

All business tended to, she escorted him upstairs and into a room decked out with its own Christmas tree in one corner, decorated tastefully with dozens of Fleur de Lis ornaments and clear lights. A large piece of metal wall art in a Fleur de Lis design hung above a king-sized bed decked out in a fluffy tan comforter. The door to a private bathroom stood ajar, revealing a large walk-in shower and a separate tub with whirlpool controls. They'd nestled a small personal refrigerator into a desk area that also held a pod-type coffee maker with a rack full of assorted coffees, teas, and cocoas. A large, overstuffed couch—perfectly designed for stretching out—rounded out the living area.

"I definitely approve." Mack stifled a yawn, heard the couch calling him for an afternoon nap. He'd been travelling for twenty-eight hours counting the two layovers at Dulles and Houston.

"If there's anything you need, feel free to let us know. Our granddaughter, Mandy, is scheduled to come in this morning—helps us out in the kitchen and with housekeeping when we need her." She checked her watch. "She may have cancelled again. That new boyfriend of hers takes precedence over us," she whispered. She smiled as her husband brought in Mack's duffel and placed it on the luggage stand.

"We'll leave you to settle in. Be sure to come down for snacks and the nightly meet and greet at 6:00 p.m. We have it early enough so that you can go out and eat at a restaurant if that's what you care to do. You're one of eight guests we have staying here tonight. But that number can change daily, of course. You and one other guest are the only two booked through Christmas and beyond."

Was that other guest escaping the ravages of winter, as well? He thanked the couple and closed the door behind them. He scanned his surroundings and, determined not to live like a drifter for the next week, emptied the contents of his duffle bag into the provided dresser drawers. He opened the fridge, picked out a bottle of juice and finished it on the comfy couch. Succumbing to the plush stuffing, he kicked off his shoes and stretched out for a short nap. The damp cool air had him shivering and he rose to look for an extra blanket, with no luck. He opened the door, met up with a young woman with an armful of bedding. Her reddish hair was pulled back into a loose ponytail and stuck out of the back opening of a black and gold New Orleans

Saints baseball cap. Obviously, the granddaughter-housekeeper.

"Excuse me, but I'll need another blanket, if you don't mind."

She faced him then, the cap's visor shielding her eyes but giving him full view of lips pursed in absolute disdain. She handed him a blanket from the stack she carried.

He thanked her, frowned as she turned her back on him and entered the room without a word. "Hmph," he grumbled. "So much for southern hospitality." He caught her turning to face him again, stiff-necked in disapproval, but closed the door on her sour expression before she could speak.

Back at the couch, he stretched out, snuggled into the soft blanket, and fell fast asleep.

* * *

Fully rested from his nap, Mack walked downstairs a few minutes shy of 6:00, hoping their idea of snacks would cure the rumbling in his stomach. He stopped, sucked in his breath at the spread before him. A long buffet table overflowed with rolls, assorted lunchmeats and cheeses, at least three types of pre-made sandwiches cut into neat triangles, and a tray full of cookies.

Drew approached carrying three large bottles of drinks, greeted him with a deep chuckle. "First one down is usually the hungriest. Grab a plate and dig in."

Mack pulled a plate from the stack and reached for a sandwich. "Don't have to tell me twice. I haven't eaten a decent meal since noon yesterday."

Beth exited a door he assumed was the kitchen, carrying another tray of pastries. "You poor thing—you must be famished."

Mack nodded. "I am, but I'm about to fix that." He bit into a chicken salad sandwich and grunted in approval.

She laughed, obviously delighted at his enthusiasm. "And FYI, our kitchen is always open. If you get the urge for leftovers or a PB & J at midnight, come on down and help yourself to whatever you find."

Drew appeared once more, this time placing an ice bucket next to the drinks. "You know, the majority of our guests drive in and have their own vehicles to get around. You didn't mention renting a car or anything—did you plan to?"

"It could happen. I wanted to get the lay of the land first. Some people's idea of secluded translates to walking distance for others."

Drew emitted a deep rumble of laughter. "We're further than walking distance. I can take you to rent something in the morning, if you'd like. Or tonight if you're in a hurry."

"Only thing I'm in a hurry to do is fill this empty spot in my belly." Mack popped the other half of the sandwich into his mouth. He filled his plate and sat at one end of a snack bar, saving the tables for the couples entering the room.

Within minutes, the place went from quiet murmurs to boisterous laughter and conversations crossing all tables. As per overheard conversations, Mack discovered that most of the couples were from nearby states, some stopping for a couple of nights on their way to New Orleans, or in the opposite direction to Texas. Another couple in their seventies had spent their last several anniversaries at the lodge. The old man had taken his wife's hand and proclaimed they planned to do so until their death, or the lodge closed, whichever came first. He ended it with a loud smack of a kiss to her lips, drawing a round of applause and one jesting "Get a room!"

The woman's reply of "We already did!" drew a second round of laughter.

"Oh, my goodness—that's what you call cuteness overload."

The velvety smooth voice at the opposite end of the bar had Mack twisting in his chair, eager to get a glimpse of the owner. "You must have snuck up on me while I wasn't looking." He reached over and extended his hand. "Hello, I'm Mack Henry."

"Natalie Bradford—and we've met." She lifted her gaze to him and her full lips twisted in smirk. "I'm a little curious to know what it was about me that made you assume I was the housekeeper."

The bite of her comment landed a direct punch to Mack's gut. "O—oh—I—I'm s—so sorry," he stammered. The pretty young woman before him bore no resemblance to the young girl with the armload of bedding. "The baseball cap thing, and your hair—you looked like a kid earlier," he admitted.  No kid here, but a woman—and a beauty, at that. Rich, auburn curls framed a heart-shaped face, adorned with a touch of make-up—just enough to highlight her high cheekbones and the brightness of inquisitive green eyes. His gaze dropped to her lips, pursed in the exact same disdainful smirk she'd worn earlier. Yeah—a dead give a way.

"Don't give it another thought." Her left eyebrow lifted in anything but amusement. "I certainly won't."

"Again, I'm so soar—"

Natalie rose from the barstool and grabbed her plate in a single fluid motion, cutting him off mid-sentence. She occupied a recently cleared table—obviously preferred eating solo over being anywhere in his vicinity.

*Message received and noted.*

He spent the next hour speaking to everyone in the room *but* the red-headed beauty. Their first icy encounter had obviously set the tone, in concrete, between them.

Later, the Brunson's invited all of them out back for a view of the stars and further fellowship around the fire-pit. Mack and the redheaded Natalie both attended, seated at the farthest point possible from each other, avoiding all eye contact. He did catch her staring into the fire at one point, the fingers of her right hand twisting the wedding band on her left ring finger. Funny he hadn't noticed it before—he usually zeroed in on the marital status of a woman instantly.

Mack called it an early night and went to his room. He opened the police thriller he'd started reading, tried to push aside thoughts of the woman across the hall. His last conscious thought had been about how to make up for his first bad impression with her—or whether it would even be worth the effort.

## Chapter 3

December 21st

Natalie waited until nearly 9:00 a.m. before heading down to breakfast the next morning, hoping to avoid her neighbor across the hall. Several people crowded around the snack bar, filling the room with the buzz of their conversations. She targeted a single remaining table in the far corner, sighed in relief when she didn't see him in the room. Hopefully, he'd eaten and headed out already. She filled her plate at the buffet and seated herself. The proprietress approached with a coffee carafe and filled her cup with the rich, aromatic brew.

"Thank you, Ms. Beth. What's with the full house this morning?"

"I asked members of the community to meet here so we could discuss final details of our annual Christmas hayride. Every year, we gather food items, frozen turkeys, and gifts for needy families in the area. We distribute them during the hayride, singing Christmas carols along the way. It's a great way to relieve the stress of holiday preparations, have some fun, and do a little good for our neighbors all at the same time. I figured since these folks came out of their way to accommodate Drew and me, the least we could do is give them a hearty breakfast."

"I haven't been on a hayride since high school. Sounds like fun," Natalie admitted.

"It was supposed to be tomorrow, but we're moving it up to tonight because of that frontal system coming through tomorrow. It won't serve any of us to catch pneumonia three days before Christmas."

"Frontal system?" Natalie asked, wide-eyed. She really should turn on the TV every now and then—if nothing else, to get the local weather report.

Beth's voice trilled with laughter. "Honey, have you been hiding under a rock the last few days? It's mild now, but by tomorrow evening we'll see the temps drop by nearly forty degrees. They're talking mid-teens by the morning of the 23rd—we could even have snow for Christmas." She paused, placed her hand on Natalie's arm. "What's the matter, honey? The weather in Biloxi isn't any different from ours."

"No—it's just that I—uh—is there a mall near here?"

"Sure. The Prien Lake Mall in Lake Charles. You need to get in some last-minute Christmas shopping?"

"Something like that." Natalie groaned inwardly. "Thanks, I'll pull it up on my car's navigational system." She sucked in her breath at the sight of Mack Henry, standing with a plate full of food and looking for an empty seat.

"Good morning, Mack!" Beth called out to him. "I'm afraid this is the last seat in the house if you don't mind sharing a table with this pretty lady, here." She looked down at Natalie. "Is that okay with you, honey?"

Natalie gave Mack the once over and swallowed. Maybe Beth's Christmas spirit rubbed off on her, but she decided it wouldn't hurt to be nice. "Sure, *mi mesa es tu mesa*." His look of confusion had her grinning. "Sit, Mr. Henry. I promise not to bite."

"You want coffee, Mack?" Beth asked, lifting her carafe.

"Yes, please." When she'd left to get him a mug, he set his plate down and sat across from Natalie. "Thanks. This is generous, considering our first meeting."

"No problem. Spirit of Christmas and all…"

He flashed a grin. "Hard not to feel it here, isn't it? I mean, this place *is* overflowing with Christmas joy, am I right?"

She smiled at the hint of laughter in his deep blue eyes. "Yeah, but I've got a feeling it's like this all year round."

His brow furrowed. "The decorations?"

"No—the good will to men and all. Judging from the reviews this place gets regularly from repeat guests, they're generally nice people."

He nodded and bit into a slice of crispy bacon. "They seem to be."

They dug into their breakfasts, nearly identical in the items they'd chosen to fill their plates. Eventually their small talk circled to the expected frontal system.

Mack's eyes grew wide at her description of the anticipated drop in temperature. "In the teens? Are you serious?"

Natalie put down her fork, swallowed her last delicious bite of sticky bun. "That's what I hear."

"Oh man, I'm gonna have to hitch a ride to the nearest car rental dealership. Then hit a department store for some warm clothes." Mack picked up a napkin and wiped his mouth. "I flew in from Minnesota yesterday but I didn't come prepared for anything that cold."

She frowned. "But Minnesota is pretty much snowed in right now, isn't it? You must have something warm."

"One set of clothes and my over coat I wore on the plane. I thought I'd be spending a week in a warmer climate so I have a duffle bag full of T-shirts. People might get sick of seeing me in the same blue and tan plaid flannel shirt the entire week."

She nodded, picturing him framed inside the doorway of his room across the hall. "Yeah, I remember seeing it." The blue had complimented his eyes beautifully. "Just before—"

He splayed his hands before him. "I know—I know—just before I mistook you for the housekeeper. But in my defense, you had an armful of linens."

She pursed her lips, looked down her nose at him. "In my defense, I hadn't recuperated from a six-hour road trip the previous night. *And* I'd just dumped a large cup of coffee on my bed. I'd gone downstairs to ask for a fresh set of linens and insisted on changing them myself."

"And you gave me your blanket."

"I did."

"Still, I shouldn't have assumed—"

She waved off his comeback. "It's forgotten. And as strange as this sounds, when it comes to being unprepared for winter storms, I bet I've got you beat."

"How so?"

"I've got nothing but a carryon full of swimwear, shorts, and sarongs."

He leaned forward, his forearms resting on either side of his empty plate. "There's a story there—I just know it."

She grinned out of one side of her mouth. "I was in the New Orleans airport, on my way to the Bahamas with my parents—not *my* idea of a Christmas vacation, but my mother wouldn't take no for an answer."

"You're from New Orleans?"

"Biloxi—we were visiting my grandmother in New Orleans before flying out. Anyway, my girlfriend called with a break up sob story and a five-day reservation for this place she wouldn't be keeping. I saw my opportunity and jumped ship—or plane."

"How convenient. Did you two have that planned?"

"No, this was Pam's Christmas gift to her fiancé. Unfortunately, she caught him with his co-worker and they split. Poor Pam couldn't face coming here, so I took it off of her hands. I turned in my ticket, hugged my folks and drove myself here in a rental."

"Were your parents upset you cancelled on them?"

"They tried to act disappointed, but I'm always a third wheel around them. Those two are still crazy about each other after closing in on forty years of marriage. It's just … nauseatingly sweet for someone in my position."

"Your position?"

She took a deep breath and released it slowly, prepared for the change—in his tone, mannerism or facial expression—once he heard her explanation. "My husband died last year."

"I'm sorry." He sounded sincere, but didn't break eye contact with her. "Was he ill?"

"In a traffic accident." Her thumb found her wedding band, spun it around on her finger.

"That's tough. Again, I'm sorry for your loss."

"Thank you. It's been—challenging." She placed her napkin on her plate and sat back. "I plan to get some shopping in at the mall in Lake Charles today."

"Could you drop me off at the nearest car rental dealership?"

"You could ride along with me. No use both of us renting a car."

"You wouldn't mind?"

"Not at all. I hate driving alone in unfamiliar cities. You could navigate for me."

He sat back, seemed to mull it over briefly before giving her a nod. "I'll buy you a tank of gas. When do we leave?"

She looked at her watch. "The mall is open, so I'm ready whenever you are."

He rose quickly and walked around the table to pull her chair out for her. "Let's hit the road, then."

* * *

By noon Natalie had put a good dent in her wardrobe deficiency. She entered the food court and located Mack amidst the noisy throng of last-minute Christmas shoppers. He saw her and approached, clutching a single large bag. "Have you eaten yet?"

"No, I didn't want to start without you." He pointed at the tiny bag in her hand. "Don't tell me that's all you bought?"

She laughed at his ludicrousness statement. "I brought mine to the car earlier after I nearly pulled a muscle lugging all my stuff." She lifted the remaining bag. "I found a booth selling hats and gloves on the way here. Let's go back to the car." She turned and started walking.

"I thought we were eating at the food court. I'm kind of hungry."

"I called Beth for the name of a good restaurant for lunch. She recommended a diner over by the bus depot—the owners are friends of theirs and Beth claims it's the best food in town from burgers to seafood."

She checked out his bag as they headed toward her car. "Did you find everything you needed? That bag doesn't look overly stuffed."

"I picked up a few more flannel shirts and a couple of pullover sweaters—I have all the jeans I needed and left Minnesota wearing my coat and boots." He shrugged. "I'm good—although I didn't think about gloves. I could use a pair."

"The booth I found had a nice selection of men's leather gloves. It's just ahead."

Mack picked up a pair of gloves and they headed to her rental. His mouthed gaped when she opened the trunk to add his bags. "You bought all that in the short time we were in there?"

She winked at him. "My shopping efficiency is exceeded only by my fabulous taste. Now let's go find that diner. I'm starved for some good Cajun cooking."

He put the diner's address in his phone's GPS and they headed out, while she explained the difference between jambalaya and etouffee.

Mack consulted his phone's screen. "Take a right on the next street. How does a girl from Mississippi know so much about Cajun food?"

"Biloxi's not far from the Louisiana border. We have several excellent Cajun restaurants there. My mom is from New Orleans and insists that most of them lean toward Creole cooking rather than Cajun. According to her and my grandmother, it's two completely different styles."

"And is she a good cook?"

"*My* mom?" Natalie hooted with laughter. "By the time I was six I'd memorized the entire McDonald's menu and knew that I preferred thin crust over pan pizza. Mom's interior design business took precedence over cooking, other than the occasional pancakes or canned biscuits and scrambled eggs for breakfasts. Now my grandmother—" She turned at the street light ahead of them. "*That* woman can cook. She can't get around in the kitchen as much now that she's in her eighties but I'd give her seafood gumbo a solid four out of four stars."

"Did she teach you?"

"I've collected quite a few recipes from her over the years." Her mind took her instantly to the last meal she'd cooked for her husband. "Craig loved my shrimp and sausage pasta—something I came up with myself—put my own spin on it, you know? Oh look, there's the diner." She filled a spot just vacated by a large SUV.

Mack got out of the car and stared at the diner. Its large painted glass window boasted *Boudreaux and Thibodeaux's* in bold lettering. "I don't have the slightest idea how to pronounce that."

"That would be *Boo-dro* and *Tib-uh-doe* and they're both common Cajun surnames."

A lovely young woman with long wavy hair and big brown eyes greeted them warmly at the door. "Welcome to Boudreaux and Thibodeaux's!"

After seating them at a table, she returned with two glasses of water and two laminated menus. "My name is Ava and I can highly recommend today's special. Our cook, Emmelia, has cooked up a batch of her crawfish corn chowder, with fresh Louisiana crawfish, of course. It's delicious, but you can order anything off of our menu."

Natalie licked her lips. "That sounds delicious, Ava. Put me down for one of those specials. Let's see what we can order for my new friend, here…" After a quick perusal of the menu, Natalie glanced at Mack. "I have two questions: do you trust me and do you have any food allergies? I don't want you blowing up like a balloon on me."

He laughed. "Yes, and no, in that order. I can eat all seafoods without looking like a puffer fish."

She ordered the seafood sampler tray for Mack and sweet tea so he could get the full south Louisiana experience.

A tall man with a bowling-ball-smooth head, stopped at the table, his hand extended toward Mack. "*Comment ca va?*" he said, in a deep, rumbling voice that seemed to match his towering height. "Or how are you if you don't speak French. I'm Pops LaCour, the owner of this establishment. I like to greet new-to-us guests. Y'all new to this area or just passing through?"

Post hand-shakes and brief introductions, Mack expounded on their situation. "Natalie and I are both staying at the Mistletoe Lodge and since we were doing some shopping in the city, the owners suggested this place for lunch."

Pop's head bobbed with enthusiasm. "Drew called me and said to expect two new faces. The wife and I have been friends with the Brunson's for a long time. You won't find better people. Is this your first time in our area?"

"I'm from Biloxi," Natalie said, "—but I've visited this area before. Mack is from Minnesota and this is his first trip to Louisiana."

"My first trip south, actually," Mack added.

Pop's eyebrows rose curiously. "The two of you aren't together? I wouldn't have guessed that. You look like you'd be a couple."

"Nope." Natalie chuckled. "It hasn't been twenty-four hours since Mack mistook me for a member of the housekeeping staff."

Pop winced visibly and faced Mack again. "Ouch! Hope you get to live that one down, buddy."

Mack grinned. "In my defense, Natalie was wearing a Saints ball cap with a pony tail and I thought she was the Brunson's teenage granddaughter."

Natalie smiled at Pops. "See how he turned that around in his favor there? How could I possibly hold that against him?"

Pops bellowed with laughter. "I guess you can't. You two have a great time in our area and we hope to see you again. Now, excuse me, please—I've got some work to do to get ready for that winter storm we're expecting."

"What a nice man!" Natalie said, facing Mack when they were alone again.

Mack sipped at his water. "Everyone's nice here. Not that people in Minnesota aren't nice. It's just...I don't know...different. People are more open around here."

"Oh, see, that's a *southern thing*, *honey*," she drawled. "Upset or insult us and you'll see the flip side of that coin."

"Please don't take this the wrong way, but I've always loved hearing women speak with a southern drawl."

"Don't tell me you Northern guys fall for the image of all Southern girls looking and speaking like Daisy Duke."

"No, but I am admitting that I think the accent is kind of sexy."

"Want me to say something else in a drawl for you?" She watched him pause, nibble on the bait before swallowing it completely.

"Uh—sure …" he murmured. "Knock yourself out." He lifted his glass of water to his mouth.

Natalie took a deep breath and closed her eyes for visual effect. "Caawwn-bread …" she drawled.

Water spewed from his mouth, followed by a coughing fit. As soon as he gained control, he burst into laughter. "I guess I should have expected that. You got me, Natalie."

She couldn't stop the laughter from bubbling over, a bit surprised at how easily it came around this guy.

He wiped his mouth, still grinning as Ava approached, bearing a tray full of food. "That can't all be for us."

"It sure is," she said, beaming as she placed a bowl of delectable smelling chowder in front of Natalie and planted a huge platter of seafood at the spot in front of Mack and pointed at different items on his plate. "That's fried shrimp and oysters, crawfish etouffee, stuffed crab and a shrimp stuffed pistolette. The two small bowls are holding samples of our seafood gumbo and chowder. Enjoy and let me know if you need anything else."

Mack popped a fried shrimp into his mouth and rolled his eyes. "Oh, that's good."

Nat downed a spoonful of chowder. "This crawfish chowder is delicious—I can honestly say it's the best I've ever had." She stared at his platter. "Think you can eat all of that?"

"I'll surely give it my best effort," he said, shoveling a forkful of etouffee into his mouth and groaning in appreciation.

They talked while they ate, each describing bits of their home lives. Two cups of coffee and two slices of pecan and coconut cream pie later, they left the diner, their bellies full, and completely at ease with each other.

\* \* \*

Mac followed 'Nat' upstairs to her room, pleased that she'd asked him to use her preferred nickname. He deposited the armload of bags on her bed and backed slowly towards the door. "Thanks again for the ride."

She smiled. "You're welcome. Hey, when I called Beth earlier, she talked me into going along with them on that hayride tonight. Are you going?"

He hadn't considered it before, but if Nat would be there … "Maybe I will."

She looked at her ringing phone. "That's my mom. I better get it or she'll send the police to my door. She's a worrier."

He lifted one hand in a farewell. "Later."

Inside his room, he removed all traces of packaging materials from his new clothes and headed downstairs with them. He found Ms. Beth straightening up in the living area. "Can you point me in the direction of a washer and dryer?"

She led him through a door at the opposite end of the kitchen. "Got some new duds?"

"Yeah, I tagged along with Natalie. I believe we're both ready for the cold front."

"It'll be chilly by tonight, but downright frigid by tomorrow evening. Poor Drew has been wrapping pipes and making sure the generators are up to speed in case of power outages. We cook and heat water with gas but have the rare problem with downed power lines due to ice build-up on branches, and our water well runs on electricity. Hopefully, the generators will keep everything running smoothly."

She started his batch of laundry washing and closed the door behind them. "If you want to come along on the hayride with us tonight, our van leaves here at 6:30 sharp."

"I'm considering it." He went up to his room, tried to read, but his mind kept flashing to thoughts of Natalie and her story. Life could certainly throw curve balls at any moment in time. His own story had proven that. Mack slammed the book shut and tossed it on the nightstand, perused the collection of coffees and cocoas. He splayed one hand over his full stomach, and turned away.

He headed downstairs, put one batch of his laundry to dry and a second batch washing then headed outside to offer Drew assistance with storm preparations.

* * *

Mack trailed Drew into the kitchen two hours later, still laughing from the lodge owner's recently delivered punch-line to a joke.

Beth looked up from pulling an oversized tray of cookies from the oven. "What's so funny?"

Engulfed by the tantalizing aroma of baked deliciousness, Mack turned to her. "Your husband's been entertaining me with his vast repertoire of Cajun jokes."

Beth placed the tray on a rack to cool and popped another into the hot oven. "He brings in the laughs at poor old Boudreaux and Thibodeaux's expense, don't you, old man?"

"His timing and delivery are impeccable—as is the accent," Mack offered. "I keep telling him he could have his own vlog and go viral."

"And I told him that sounds like something that requires a trip to the doctor, so no thank you!" Drew planted a kiss on his wife's cheek then pulled back. "Mack here was just telling me that Minnesota has its own version of Boo and Thib, but it's an old married couple named Ole and Lena."

Beth laughed. "Speaking of old married couples did you and Nat visit Pops and Lena Mae's diner today?"

Mack rubbed his belly. "We did and thanks for the recommendation. That was some mighty good eating."

"Speaking of good eating—" Drew reached for a tray of cookies.

Beth slapped her husband's hand away and lifted her finger in warning. "Doc said to watch your sugar intake, Andrew Madison!"

Mack slapped a hand on Drew's shoulder. "The situation must be serious. She pulled the big-gun-middle-name on you."

"Serious, my big toe! My sugar is just fine," Drew grumbled. He waited until she turned her back on him to steal a cookie and hit the door.

"They'll be cutting off that big toe one day when you lose circulation in it!" Beth called out as he scurried from the room. She released her breath in a huff, faced

Mack and shook her head. "I've been struggling for five years to keep his borderline diabetic status from crossing over into a full-blown case of insulin dependency. He's a hard sell, that's for darn sure."

Mack leaned over the cookies and breathed in the aroma. "He says your baking makes it impossible to resist, and I'm beginning to see why. I hope these are for us?"

"I'm making goodies for after the hayride tonight." She used a spatula to lift a cookie from the tray and handed it to him on a napkin. "I call these my loaded chocolate mint cookies. Nothing's better with a cup of hot cocoa—warms and satisfies at the same time."

He bit into it, his mouth exploding with a combination of chocolate, crunchy peppermint and pecan pieces mingling with the buttery sweet goodness of the chewy cookie. "Poor Drew—" he groaned. "Now I know what he's talking about." He finished the rest of it off in one bite. "It's probably a combination of your vigilance and him working hard around here that keeps him healthy."

She continued sliding the cooled cookies from one tray to a large container. "Yes, but when he retires for good, I told him he'll have to join a gym or change his eating habits. He insists that either one of those would take all the fun out of living, so what's the point?" Beth lowered her spatula and stared ahead. "But I surely can't imagine my life without him in it." She straightened and lifted her chin, as though shaking off any morose thoughts, and continued her work.

He remembered his new clothes and headed for the laundry room until she stopped him.

"It's all tended to. Everything's folded or hung in your closet." She looked up from her work. "It's the least I could do since you helped out Drew. Maybe we should be paying you to stay here."

"Thank you, but I sleep better at night if I keep busy during the day."

Beth smiled at him. "Remember, the van leaves at 6:30—I'd hate to see you miss out on an opportunity to have some fun."

"I'll be there." He headed for the stairway, his step a little lighter. If Nat planned to go, he would too.

## Chapter 4

The carolers finished their final rendition of "Jingle Bells" as an older couple with three small children stood in the doorway of their home and clapped. Dozens of farewells later, the group headed back to the sixteen-foot trailer lined on both sides with rectangular bales of hay, layered with various quilts and blankets.

Natalie stood back, patiently waited her turn to mount as Beth explained the last couple's current situation.

"Their only daughter and her husband were taken from them in a boating accident this past summer and they're raising their three grandchildren. It's such a tragedy." She clucked her tongue. "Just enough life insurance to bury them and pay off their debts. The Guidry's were making it fine on their retirement income. But Mr. James has since had to take a job as a security officer down at the court house."

Natalie frowned. "The children get social security checks, surely."

"They refuse to touch any of it—put everything straight into savings for them. Ms. Mary has her hands full with the two youngest ones but insists she wouldn't have it any other way."

Natalie turned back, studied the modest wood frame home on a corner lot—well-maintained from the looks of it. Someone had found the time to adorn the porch with colored lights and a bevy of Christmas decorations. She knew that kind of loss, respected the effort it took to keep the Christmas spirit for their grandchildren.

"You coming, Nat?"

She turned, faced a somber Mack who held his hand out to help her up onto the platform. She took his hand and stepped up. The two of them occupied the last two seats on a single hay bale.

Mack pulled the heavy quilt over their legs. "Sad story, huh? Now I know why Drew said they were saving the best house for last."

"Those poor babies." It took an effort not to release the words on a sob. "It's their first Christmas without parents." She shook her head. "Almost makes me glad Craig and I didn't have children." *Almost.* If they had, at least she'd have a part of him left, but to raise a child alone …

"Single parenting can't be easy."

She blinked at his insightful comment. "That's exactly what I was thinking."

"But did you see their little faces light up when they saw those gifts? It's like my old gramps used to say— you haven't seen Christmas until you've seen it through the eyes of a child."

"No doubt." How different would her life be if she had a child or two? Deep in contemplation, his gentle nudge to her shoulder shook her from her thoughts. She glanced up into his concerned face. "Sorry, did you say something?"

"I didn't want you to get lost in thoughts of what might have been. I've learned when I do that, I sometimes miss out on what's happening now."

Natalie allowed herself another minute to detach herself from those feelings before she rejoined the singing for the ride back to the lodge. She listened to other conversations around her, but kept her thoughts and comments to herself until they reached their destination.

The Brunson's big yellow dog bounded off the porch, his tail wagging gleefully. "There's old Duke—our welcoming committee!" Drew called out.

Mack exited first and bent over to ruffle Duke's coat. He straightened and extended his hand to Natalie. "Let me help you off the trailer."

She smiled and stepped down, pulled her hand out of his as soon as her foot hit solid ground. Beth invited everyone into the Lodge for cookies and hot cocoa. Some of the carolers begged off, claiming to have things to tend to, either pertaining to the approaching cold front or other family gatherings. Others joined them inside. A few left shortly after, armed with goody bags of cookies.

"Who's joining us out back at the fire pit tonight?" Drew called to the guests. "It could be our last chance before Christmas. This should be the last mild evening we have for the next several days."

"I'm there!" Mack turned his smiling face to Natalie. "How about you, Nat? You up for some S'mores around the fire pit?"

She placed her hand over her belly. "I'm too full for S'mores, but I'm always up for a good campfire."

Drew had the pit logs blazing within minutes while a dozen people circled chairs around the iron pit on the stone paved patio. The colored Christmas lights along the roofline competed with the dancing light of the flames, casting a cozy glow over the faces in the circle. The lights were dim enough not to interfere with the display of stars scattered against the velvety blackness of the night sky.

Mack occupied the vacant chair beside Natalie. She studied his handsome face in the firelight, the blue of his eyes darkened by shadows. "You know *my* story, Mack—so what's yours?"

He released his breath in a rush. "Not much to tell. I chose an Army career over college out of high school. I left the Army when we lost my dad to a massive stroke six years later. I'm the only child and my mom needed me home."

"And …" Natalie prodded, wanting more.

"And that's it. I've cared for my mom, worked, and dug us both out of the snow for the last twelve Minnesota winters."

A quick mental calculation put his age at or around thirty-six. "No time for a wife or girlfriend?"

"I've had two fiancées. The first one called it off—decided she could do better. I called the second one off after realizing I'd been going through the motions. She deserved better—deserved someone who truly loved her." He stretched out his long legs. "I haven't met anyone else who's made me want to put myself out there like that again." He faced her. "Now you know I've never been married and I know you've got a soft heart when it comes to children." He paused a few seconds. "How long were you and your husband together?"

She took a deep breath and dove in. "We met our senior year of college, dated for two years, and married for eight." She blinked several times. "The accident happened a year ago—from today."

"Oh." He opened his mouth, closed it again. "I'm sorry for bringing—"

She raised her hand to cut him off. "I started this line of questioning—it's only fair. Besides, I'm better than I thought I'd be at this point." She leaned forward in her chair. "I still miss Craig so badly, but just after it happened—I couldn't imagine life without him."

"Anyone who truly loves their spouse must feel that way."

She settled back in her chair, crossed her arms tightly against her chest. "I can't speak for anyone else, but I struggled with it, to the point that anger began to replace pain."

"That's a universal stage in the grieving process. Everyone experiences anger at their loved ones for leaving them."

She placed one hand on her chest. "My anger was with God. How dare he take away my husband? How *dare* he? I was furious and ready to toss out all my spiritual beliefs. Then I heard some preacher say that God tests us by bringing storms into our lives. Whether it's in the form of a death, or temptation, or coveting—

He will test us in order to assess our commitment to Him."

Mack nodded. "I believe that. I've seen it happen many times. I've seen some stand up to it, and others fall on their faces. Men and women who had everything they needed in life then lost it all for various reasons—everything from addictions to adultery. There's no winner."

Natalie faced him. "Right? It's easy to think you're a good person—a Godly person, even—if everything has always gone your way. It's only when people are *tested* that the truth is revealed."

"So that was your 'Aha' moment?"

"I guess so—that's when I began to pull myself up a day at a time. Every morning I'd wake and tell myself to identify at least one good thing about each day. Every night I'd think back and find something and realized those good things had been there all along." Her gaze locked on to his. "That's when I began to live again."

He reached over as though he were going to place his hand on hers, stopped in mid-motion and clasped his two hands together instead, staring into the fire. "I'm certainly glad you did."

Duke sidled over to her, looking for some attention. She leaned forward in her chair and cradled the dog's large golden head in her two hands. "How old are you, boy?"

Mack cleared his throat. "Drew told me he's twelve years old."

"Well, let's hope you have a few more left in you, Duke." The dog edged closer to her to lay his head on her thigh. She leaned forward and hugged him. "You are just a loveable guy, aren't you?"

"I could be with the right person."

She chuckled without looking up at Mack. "I was talking to the dog. I don't know you well enough to make that call." For several seconds she wished she did—wanted to get to know him well enough to decide for herself. *He lives in Minnesota.* That translated to nada...zilch...zero benefit in pursuing any kind of relationship with the man. She couldn't abide two things—long distance relationships and prolonged stretches of extreme cold. Wouldn't you know the first man to catch her interest since she lost Craig was a walking poster child for the impossible.

"Look what I found lying around on the ground!"

Natalie looked up as Beth approached the group holding a cluster of dark green foliage. "What is that?"

Drew stood and reached for his wife's prize. "That is the culprit that gave this place one half of its name. You've seen our view of the sky—our own Southern Lights. *This* is a small portion of the mistletoe that grows in the oaks around here." He took the cluster from Beth and held it over his wife's head, then leaned in to give her a quick kiss. A spattering of applause had Beth covering her face. Drew winked at Mack. "See? I told you, everything has its place in this world—even a parasite like mistletoe."

By 11:00 p.m. the crowd had thinned out to a few stragglers. Natalie entered the lodge and immediately took the stairs to her room. She paused at her door when Mack called out from down the hall.

"I have a little souvenir for you." He approached, holding a small cluster of mistletoe with a bright red ribbon tied to the stem for hanging. "Ms. Beth said to make sure you got this."

"Cool." She reached for it, but he pulled it away.

"Not so fast. She insists they have a strict tradition about the transference of mistletoe around here."

"Oh, yeah?" She stood waiting, hands on her hips. "This should be good."

He nodded and held the beribboned cluster over his own head. "Tradition demands that whoever takes it off my hands has to give me a kiss or they'll have bad luck for a week."

"Is that right?"

"That's the word."

"Well, I surely don't need a week's worth of bad luck." Natalie stepped forward and faced him before standing on her tippy toes. "Close your eyes." He did, and she kissed him on his left cheek, before reaching up to grab the mistletoe out of his hands. "Thanks!" She spun quickly on her heels and entered her room. "Goodnight, Mack. See you tomorrow." Closing the door on his astonished face, she giggled at his mild grumbling from the hallway.

"You don't play fair, lady," he called out from the hallway. "But have a good night anyway."

"You too," she countered. Nat leaned against her door until she heard his door open and shut. Smiling, she studied the leafy green cluster before placing it on her nightstand. The smile remained through her hot shower, and long after she'd snuggled under the flannel sheets and thick comforter on her soft bed.

## Chapter 5

December 22nd

Beth turned, coffee carafe in hand, and smiled when Mack entered the otherwise empty dining room. "Good morning, Mack. You're a little early but I'll have the buffet laid out in ten minutes."

He returned her smile. "That's fine. I'll need to finish a cup before I eat, anyway."

She walked to the table nearest the large window overlooking the side yard, carafe in hand. "First in gets the best table in the house. Did you sleep well?"

"Thanks." Mack met her at the table, stretched his arms over his head and tried to smother a yawn. "I slept fine." *Liar*. Truth be told, he'd slept fitfully, with thoughts of Natalie running through his mind. He'd lain awake for an hour, pondered the emotional connection he felt to the woman. It didn't matter if they were eyeballs deep in a discussion or silently occupying the same space. Being around Nat came easier to him than it had after months of dating either of his two former fiancées.

He thought about the encounter with Nat last night at the door to her room—had he gone too far with his little mistletoe stunt? Would she even want to spend time with him? He stared out the window at the rope swing descending from a large branch of the massive oak. It sat completely still with the absence of any kind of breeze.

Beth lifted a coffee mug from the table's place setting and filled it. "Do you have anything special planned for today?"

"What's the news on that cold front?"

"It won't make it here until later this evening. You've got the entire day to sight see while the weather permits. Drew and I were wondering if you'd ever seen the Gulf."

He lifted the mug to his nose and breathed in the rich aroma. "I haven't. Is it far from here?"

"An hour and some change, and you'll get to see some Louisiana marshland along the way, maybe even an alligator or two sunning themselves. It's something to think about, right?"

"Minnesota has plenty of marshland but I've never seen an alligator in its natural habitat." He sipped the hot coffee, closing his eyes as it slid down his throat. "Man, this is good stuff. Can I get it up in Wisconsin?"

Beth shook her head. "Not this particular blend. It's my secret." The door opened and a group of four men entered the dining room. "I'll be with you gentlemen in a minute. Go ahead and seat yourselves."

One man pulled out a chair at the table nearest the door and sat. "We'll all take our usual orders, Beth."

"Sure thing, Kip." Beth leaned over and winked at Mack. "My coffee's been bringing in the regulars for ten years. These fellas are all local, could just as easily drink their own coffee from their own kitchens, yet they come here for breakfast and at least three mugs each. Part of what keeps this place in the black all year long."

He took another sip, knowing he'd never find anything this good off the grocery store shelves back home. "Could I talk you out of your secret?"

"Nope. I decided way back when I created the blend that I'd only reveal it to the next owner of this place—it's only fair." She leaned in close. "I know Drew's ready to sell, but I've been putting him off until the right person comes along." She left him with a wink, approached the second table and filled the men's four coffee mugs before disappearing into the kitchen.

Mack nursed his coffee, contemplating her words until a feminine voice broke into his thoughts.

"Care for some company?"

Startled, he looked into Natalie's smiling face. "Absolutely!" He stood to pull out the chair next to his, rather than across from him. To his delight, she took it without hesitation.

Beth appeared like magic, again bearing the carafe and her usual bright smile. "Good morning, Natalie. Will you both be eating from the buffet, or would you like to try something from our breakfast menu this morning? I'm whipping up a batch of my French toast recipe for my regulars over there, if either of you would like to try it."

Natalie's eyes lit up and she clasped her hands together. "Could I have powdered sugar sprinkled on mine?"

Beth grinned and placed a hand on Natalie's arm. "I'll hook you up, honey." She faced Mack. "How about it, Mack? Want to add French toast to your Louisiana experiences?"

Mack swallowed his coffee and set down his mug. "I grew up eating my mom's recipe but I'll try yours for comparisons' sake." He watched Beth disappear into the kitchen again, faced Natalie when she spoke.

"The Minnesota version of French toast may differ a little from the southern version. I hope you're not disappointed."

He grinned at her, decided to divulge a little info about his heritage. "I haven't mentioned this yet, but my mom is actually from this area of Louisiana. She was a Landry before she married my dad. I read the other day that Landry is the second most common Cajun name in Louisiana."

Her eyes wide with surprise, she sat back in her chair. "I never would have guessed you had roots here.

So, if Landry is the second most common, what's the first?"

"It's pronounced *A-bear*, but spelled H-E-B-E-R-T."

Natalie poured a little creamer in her coffee and added a spoonful of sugar. "I'm familiar with the name and I don't doubt that. My best friend married an *A-bear* from the Lafayette area. We do lunch or a movie at least once a month and she's always saying how the families pack the rental hall for their reunions." She stirred her coffee. "So, is that why you decided to come down to Louisiana for the holidays—to get in touch with your Cajun roots? And how about your mom—did she come too?"

"I came alone. My mom won an all-inclusive trip for two to Hawaii through a local radio station. She and her first cousin, Margaret, grew up more like sisters than cousins. That's who she took with her to Hawaii. They met up in California and flew together from there."

Natalie grinned at him. "Did she ask you first to go with her?"

He nodded. "And as much as I love my mom, I had no desire to spend two solid weeks with her. Cousin Margaret was her next choice. When mom told Margaret that I wanted to come south to get out of the snow for a while, she suggested I look up this place." He looked up as Beth approached with two platters of French toast. "I think you and my mom's cousin Margaret went to school together didn't you, Ms. Beth?"

Beth placed one platter on the table and paused. "There were a couple of Margaret's in my class…which one?"

Mack tore his attention away from the platter of delectable delights before him to meet her curious gaze. "Margaret is a Miller now, but her maiden name was Suire. My mom was a Landry."

"Margaret Suire's cousin …" Her eyes widened in a moment of clarity. "Don't tell me you're Marie Landry's boy."

"I am."

She slapped her free hand over her chest. "I can't believe it! Why didn't you say something before?"

He shrugged. "Would it have made a difference? I can't imagine you treating me any better than you already have."

She placed a hand on his wrist and smiled. "That's sweet of you to say." She pointed to the second table full of men. "Let me get this to those guys and I'll be back."

Natalie forked two slices of French toast onto her plate, leaned over and closed her eyes to breathe it in. "Mm, smell that vanilla and cinnamon…looks just like my grandma's." She cut a tiny piece and popped it into her mouth, groaning in appreciation. "Delicious!" She waited until she'd finished a bigger bite before commenting. "It's a small, world, huh?"

"It's not like it's a coincidence, since Margaret is the one who suggested this place." He looked up as Beth approached their table again.

"Now that I know you're Marie's boy, I'm wondering why I didn't see it before. You favor her." Beth's eyes softened as she smiled. "It makes perfect sense now—it's why you fit in here so well."

"Thanks, I'll take that as a compliment."

"That's exactly how I meant it." She pointed at his plate. "That should taste just like your mom's. Your grandmother is the one who taught us all how to make it. The three of us spent most of our summers together all during junior high and high school."

Mack sliced off a piece and toast and speared it with his fork to pop it into his mouth. He chewed and swallowed before speaking again. "It's exactly like my mom's. And it's got the perfect amount of crisp to it. Do you use a black iron frying pan?"

She nodded. "Your grandmother insisted it was the only way to make proper French toast." She sat back and perused the two of them. "You know, Natalie— Mack here was telling me earlier that he's never seen the Gulf of Mexico before. Maybe the two of you could take a ride down to the beach. Hurricane Rita turned that entire coastal area of Cameron Parish into a blank canvas back in 2005—so many homes and business destroyed. It's made a huge comeback."

Natalie used a napkin to wipe her mouth. "Rita did as much damage here as Katrina did in Biloxi. I grew up on the Gulf coast, and I've vacationed on beaches all along the Mississippi and Alabama coastline, as well as the Florida panhandle. I've never seen any of Louisiana's beaches so I'm game." She picked up her phone and checked the time. "We're a little over an hour from the coast so if we leave now, we can be back to watch some football."

The two of them dug into their meal, making plans for the rest of their day.

Beth brought them more coffee and dropped off a stack of brochures describing and laying out routes of the Creole Nature Trail. "Whichever route you decide to take, make sure you travel via the Gibbstown Bridge over the Intracoastal Waterway at least once. I've always loved the view from there."

They thanked her and studied the brochures, heads bent in concentration. They looked up when Drew walked over, rapped his knuckles on the table to get their attention.

"Beth tells me you're headed down to the beach today. Y'all be careful and make sure you get back in plenty of time. They say that storm front's going to be a real doozy."

Mack sat up straight in his chair. "Any suggestions on which route to take?"

"If your goal is to see the beach, I'd avoid the west end—too much traffic congestion coming off that I-10 Bridge. Take 14 down to the Gibbstown Bridge and head straight to Rutherford Beach."

Natalie gathered the brochures. "Sounds good to me."

"Enjoy that drive while you can because the city has east end expansion projects in the works. Five years from now that end will be just as congested as the west end with shopping centers and traffic lights. Besides, the beach looks the same from one end to another. It's not like you're going in for a dip." His right brow arched comically. "Unless you've lost your senses, because that water is going to be colder than a well-digger's behind."

Nat shook her head. "Not me."

"Nope," Mack added before facing Natalie. "I guess we've decided on our route then. I'm ready when you are."

*Chapter 6*

Natalie and Mack took the route their hosts suggested and headed south on Highway 14. They passed several subdivisions along the way, all part of the city of Lake Charles' recent eastward expansion Drew mentioned, each one boasting large beautiful homes.

Mack whistled through his teeth at the structures. "I doubt if the price tag for a single one of those is under a million bucks."

"So how does this area differ from where you live?"

"Topography wise, you mean? If you had six feet of snow covering everything in sight, it'd look pretty much the same. TRF's terrain is every bit as flat as this." He went into further explanation at Nat's raised brow. "I live in a small city named Thief River Falls—Thief River or TRF for short."

"What an odd name. Do you know its origin?"

"The short version is that before white man ever set foot there, a Sioux warrior murdered a member of the Chippewa tribe. The warrior hid out at the river for years, evaded capture even though surrounded by his enemy. He survived by stealing and pillaging. At some point, the Chippewa associated the river's name with the Sioux thief's presence and the English translation turned into Thief River."

"So, there's a river somewhere in your city, right?"

"Two, actually; the Thief River joins with the Red Lake River. There are thousands of lakes in Minnesota—"

"Isn't it called the land of ten thousand lakes?"

"That's right. But we have rivers in our area with lots of river front property. No mountainous terrain in the northwest corner of our state and no beaches."

Natalie cocked her head to one side. "Minnesota is in this same time zone as we are, right? Only we're separated by, what is it, four states?"

"Only three states from Louisiana—those being Iowa, Missouri, and Arkansas. Did I mention we're only eighty miles from the Canadian border?"

"I've never been to Canada, but it's on my bucket list." Nat adjusted the volume on the car's radio. "I used to think I'd love living in the mountains. Then we spent

Christmas at a lodge up in the mountains and every time I tried to drive anywhere, I got lost. Those mountain roads terrified me at night." She waved her hands. "No thank you. I'll stay down south."

"Have you ever been on a cruise?"

Her mouth twisted in a grimace. "Only once, on our honeymoon, but poor Craig stayed sea-sick the first three days. We should have booked a bigger boat."

Mack told her about his trips to the Grand Canyon and Mount Rushmore. They started up a large bridge as he was repeating the tale of how he'd been locked out of a hotel room in his underwear. He grinned as Natalie cracked up at his description of coming face to face with an old woman on the way to ask for another room key.

"Boxers or briefs?" she managed to snort out.

"Does it really matter? I mean, at least I was covered …" He stopped mid-sentence when their car crested the bridge. "This must be that Gibbstown Bridge Beth and Drew talked about. Look at all that marshland. She was right about the view."

Natalie agreed, her tone somewhat stiff. Matt glanced over, noticed her fingers curled tightly on the steering wheel. He waited until she'd reached the bottom of the bridge before asking about her white knuckled clench. "A buddy of mine back home has a phobia and can't drive over bridges. You okay?"

Natalie flexed her fingers, somewhat loosening her grip. "My phobia is being surrounded by water in a vehicle."

"Can't swim?"

"I'm not a strong swimmer and I dreamed once I was in a car that drove off the side of a roadway into a large body of water." She gave her head a quick shake. "I woke up terrified and driving near water has bothered me since then. I figure it was God giving me a warning." Her mouth twisted in a half smile. "Or maybe it was indigestion—"

"A bit of undigested beef or a fragment of uncooked potato?"

She cast a sideways glance at him. "Did somebody watch that old version of *A Christmas Carol* last night?"

"Sure did." He shrugged. "I couldn't sleep and it was my favorite version. I'd offer to take the wheel, but since it's a rental…"

She waved off his offer. "No, I'm fine. I refuse to let it control me, so I push myself to drive in situations like this."

He nodded, admiring her nerve. Truth be told, he admired a lot about the lady. He faced the roadway again, focused on something up ahead of them. "Is that what I think it is?"

She chuckled and checked her mirror to make sure they weren't being followed before pulling slowly to a stop. Several yards ahead of them, an alligator sunned itself on the side of the road, half in and half out of the grassy shoulder area between the canal and roadway. "Is this your first alligator?"

"In its natural habitat," he admitted. "Look at that thing! He doesn't seem threatened by us, does he?"

She laughed. "Why should he be? He knows if we get out and approach him, all he has to do is turn those big ugly teeth our direction and we'd high tail it back to the safety of these four wheels. Besides, he's sound asleep."

Mack opened his car door. "I've got to get a closer look. You coming?"

"Uh—no! You go ahead, crazy man. I'm better off with several thousand pounds of steel and four wheels between me and that prehistoric creature. Hurry before another vehicle comes along and has to drive around us."

Mack took several cautious steps toward the animal, his phone in hand, camera app ready to get a picture. He'd taken several shots of the gator—then zoomed in close for some video when the animal opened its eyes. Its huge head turned slowly toward him. The gator let out a short, low grunt and whipped its long tail toward him.

"Okay, big fella—I'll leave you to your business." Mack headed for the car, his gait unhurried until Natalie blew the horn, waving her hands frantically, and called out through her open window to "Run!"

He sprinted to the car without looking back and jumped inside, his heart thundering in his chest.

She placed her hand on his arm, her eyes wide with alarm. "That was so close, Mack—he nearly got you!"

He craned his neck out of his passenger window trying to find the gator—eventually found it—in the exact same spot ahead of them. He turned slowly to face his chauffeur. Only then did Nat remove the hand she had clamped over her mouth, bursting into raucous laughter. He waited until her snorts transitioned into quiet chuckles. "You took five years off of my life, and don't seem a bit sorry."

She wiped tears of laughter from her eyes. "If you're crazy enough to get that close to a live gator for a *picture*, you had it coming. You could have taken the same shots from the safety of the car."

"That thing never moved from his spot," he protested.

"But he could have. Don't let that log-like appearance fool you. Those things can move fast when they want to and people can trip over their own feet trying to get out of their way. Next thing you know, the gator's got those jaws clamped around an ankle or leg and it's performing that 'death roll' in the water with its prey."

He placed his hand over his chest, willing his heartbeat to return to normal. "I'll give you that one. Lesson learned."

She put the car in drive. "It would have been a shame for you to come all the way down here just to become gator take-out."

She made a valid point, but Mack focused his gaze outside his window rather than admit it. "I recognize some of the same types of water plants that we have up in our own lakes and marshes—cattails, lilies, duckweed—I guess that stuff will grow anywhere." They drove on with a large canal running parallel to the right side of the road. Marshland stretched out on both sides, some crowded with what Nat called salt grass.

They got to an intersection and stopped in front of a small store boasting a sign that read "T-Boy's". Mack gave Nat a curious look.

"It's a Cajun thing," she explained. "When you see 'T' in front of anything, it generally means little as in the French word for small being *petite*. The French don't usually pronounce the 'p' in the word, so it comes out 'teet' and generally sounds like 'tee'." She shrugged. "My gran's explanation, anyway."

He nodded and they drove further south where the homes gradually transitioned to stilted structures, raised to avoid the inevitable storm surges. They took a left at the next intersection, passed a high school and several nice homes in the area. He waved at a young woman digging in a flower bed in front of one of the homes, a little boy with blond curls playing in the yard beside her.

Mack checked his phone's GPS. "I think we're going in the wrong direction. We were supposed to turn right back there." They doubled back and eventually turned south at a road sign that read Rutherford Beach. An ever-present canal accompanied the two-lane paved road on one side. Mack stared out across the grassy marsh to the north, could see the school they'd just passed on the opposite side.

After a few winding turns his breath caught at his first glimpse of the gulf. "That's beautiful."

Natalie parked near a small picnic area with a covered slab housing four concrete picnic tables and a couple of grills for public use. Four port-a-potties, aligned in a row like multicolored sentinels, stood to the north of the area, across a wide patch of sand.

Mac got out of the car first, stopped in front of a large post with several multi-colored wooden signs tacked vertically to the surface. Its message, reading from top to bottom over six rough pieces of wood— *Please leave nothing but your footprints*—a constant reminder to all visitors not to litter. He walked across a stretch of loose, dry sand to reach the compact wet sand at the water's edge.

Waves crashed around him as far as he could see, white with froth. Both excited and lulled by the constant battering of waves and surf, he looked up as the cry of a gull pierced the air. He followed the bird's flight across the beach, watched it glide gracefully and land several yards away.

Mack scanned the deserted beach, it's not quite white sand littered only with occasional pieces of driftwood and thousands of small colorful shells. He saw beach houses of different colors, shapes, and sizes far to the right, all stilted.

Natalie appeared at his side. "It's not quite clear enough to see all of them, but I bet there are dozens of oil drilling platforms out there." She pointed to a couple of the closest rigs, barely visible through the mist and cloudy conditions. "Still, it's beautiful, isn't it?"

"It is," he agreed.

"I never get tired of looking at it." She took a step forward and picked up a perfectly shaped seashell, blended with purples and pinks. "Here, a souvenir from your trip south."

Mack and Nat spent the next hour walking the deserted strip of beach slowly, from one end to the other. Head to head, they stood in one spot and compared their cache of seashells. A child's laughter cut through the air, drawing their attention to a couple walking with a toddler.

"Aw, look at that beautiful little girl, Mack. I wonder if this is her first trip to the beach."

Her tone, a strange combination of joy and sadness, prodded his curiosity. "I've never been married, Nat, so no children for me. But you were, for eight years. I bet you'd make a great mom, so why don't you have any?"

She sucked in her lips and closed her eyes. "We tried. For years we tried. Tests determined I was okay." She took a deep breath, as though she needed to fortify herself for the rest of her speech. "Craig would have been fine with no children, but I wanted them so badly.

So …" She paused to swallow. "He—he was on his way to a clinic to have tests run when—when it happened." She blinked several times and wiped at her eyes. "There's this small part of me that feels—I don't know—if I hadn't wanted children so badly, maybe…"

He grasped at her hand, clutched it between both of his. Her fingers had already turned cold in the chill of the moist gulf breeze whipping off the water. "Don't do that to yourself, Nat. You have no way of knowing what would have happened. My dad would have died from his stroke whether I'd have been there or not. People leave us when it's their time."

Natalie placed her free hand on his chest and looked up into his face, her green eyes sparkling with unshed tears. "I do know that in my heart. I know Craig wouldn't have wanted me to feel any kind of guilt over what happened. It sill creeps in."

Mack waited until she lowered her head before wrapping his arms around her. He held her there, hugging, swaying slowly in the breeze, surrounded by the mesmerizing sounds of the surf. They parted eventually, and began the slow walk back toward the car, their fingers linked lightly. They reached the car and broke the contact, each retreating to their own side.

Mack closed the door on the sounds of the gulf waters. The absence left him with an empty feeling, and he realized he missed both the sound and the touch of her fingers linked in his. They drove back to the lodge with the radio tuned low to a country station, each too wrapped up in their own thoughts to carry on any kind of meaningful conversation.

They arrived back at the lodge by noon, just in time to join the Brunson's in front of the living area's 70" flat screen to watch the Saints at Titans football game. In the presence of three Saints fans, Mack got wrapped up in their enthusiasm—he found himself cheering at their win.

Mack retreated to his room afterwards, sat alone in silent reflection of the day. Images of Natalie at the beach replayed in his mind. Had he done the right thing by prodding her the way he had—when clearly, he'd reopened old wounds, brought her to tears? Maybe he should have apologized. He could next time he saw her, but that would bring it all back and he didn't want her revisiting that pain.

How would Nat have reacted if he'd taken his impulse to hold her a single step further? What would she have done if he'd kissed her on that beach? He'd wanted to—had resisted the urge. He dropped his head heavily on the back of the overstuffed chair, wondering if he'd been a fool to let the opportunity pass him by.

## Chapter 7

Craving some alone time after the Saints win, Natalie retreated to her room. By 4:00 pm, the skies had darkened with ominous clouds. She sat with her book club's choice of the month, tossed it aside after several more unengaged flips of the page, and turned on her lamp. Restless, she approached the window and caught sight of several guests loading up their cars to leave. Drew and Mack hauled cases of something from Drew's pickup truck to the back door of the lodge. Her curiosity piqued, she headed downstairs.

She entered the kitchen area, assaulted by a combination of delectable baked good aromas and whatever simmered on the commercial stove top. "Mercy, it smells good in here. What are you cooking?"

Beth turned from stirring a large pot, her face wreathed with her usual smile. "I figure nobody wants to be out driving around searching for supper in the ugly weather about to hit us. So, I whipped up a batch of vegetable beef soup. I'll serve it with thick slices of homemade bread and crackers."

Nat lifted her nose to the air and sniffed. "I smell vanilla."

"That would be my buttermilk pies in the oven. It's an egg custard pie that always goes over big with my guests." She checked her timer and spun around; her fingers clasped tightly together. "This weather has got me as jittery as a mouse in a roomful of hungry tomcats. When I'm nervous, I bake."

Nat strolled over to several platters of cookies set out on the length of counter top. "You must be plenty nervous. What do we have here—chocolate chip, oatmeal raisin, more of those yummy peppermint ones—and hold up—are these what I think they are?"

Beth approached, reached for a cookie and handed it to her. "*These* are my weakness."

Nat bit into the crunchy decadence, her eyes closed, as flavors exploded and rolled around in her mouth until she'd swallowed it down. "White chocolate-macadamia is my favorite cookie—I thought I'd tasted the best, but

…" She faced Beth. "There's something else in this that takes it a step above. What's your secret?"

Beth put her finger to her lips and winked. "For your ears and eyes only, because something tells me I can trust you to keep it to yourself." She reached into a canister and pulled out a storage bag of candy bars—all of them chocolate covered toffee. "I process a few of these babies into fine pieces and mix it into the batter. I find it adds so much to the flavor."

Nat finished off the rest of the cookie and wiped the crumbs from her fingers before crossing her heart. "I'll never tell. Now, in thanks, what can I do to help?"

The air rang with Beth's laughter. "You and Mack—the two of you are a pair. Everyone else is grumbling about the approaching weather, as though we could prevent it from disrupting anyone's plans. But you two are offering to help rather than asking for refunds."

As if the mention of his name conjured him up, the back door swung open and Mack appeared, trailed by Drew, each carrying cases of water. Mack glanced up, caught her eye for the briefest of seconds before both men deposited the water in the large pantry area.

Drew exited the pantry, wiping his hands on his jeans. "That's the last of it, Beth. There's enough water there to bathe half the city of Lake Charles." He winked at Natalie. "It won't hurt the other half to stink for a bit."

Beth stared at the boxes piled in neat stacks inside her pantry. "I suppose it'll do."

Natalie stood beside the proprietress. "I thought you had a generator if the electricity to the water well cut off."

"We do," Drew insisted. "I like to prepare for the unexpected." He looked toward the back porch as the wind picked up, knocking over one of Beth's plant stands. "We better get those plants to the back shed if you don't want to lose 'em, honey. Gotta take care of the three P's in freezing weather—plants, pipes, and pets."

Natalie followed the two men onto the back porch. "I'll help carry some plants for you, Drew."

Drew pointed out a potted fern. "Grab that one, and we'll get the others. Thanks for helping, Natalie. You and Mack are two in a million."

"No problem." Nat grabbed the fern then looked around. "Speaking of protecting pets, where's Duke?"

"Old Duke took a trip to the groomers earlier this afternoon. He got a bath and a good combing, so he gets to sleep inside for however long it takes the temps to get back to normal. He's too old to be out in the cold."

They arranged the half-dozen potted plants in two neat rows in a shed every bit as organized as Beth's pantry. Natalie pointed to laminated labels tacked onto wooden shelving. "Is this your handiwork?"

Drew's chuckle rumbled like an old boat motor in the small space. "That's all Beth. She couldn't stand my method of organization. I generally just stand at the door and toss whatever it is as far as I can until it lands. It was a real mess until she came in and worked her magic."

Mack stood next to Nat, perusing the shelves. "But you seem to be doing a good job of keeping it up."

Drew grinned, his eyes crinkled in amusement. "She said I'd better if I didn't want to face the consequences. I don't have the nerve to push her on it. My girl thrives on organization."

Natalie trailed Mack back toward the house while Drew closed up the shed. She stopped beside him as he pointed upward.

"Look at that cloud formation, would you, Nat?"

"I love winter storms. This one's nearly on top of us." She turned, caught him staring at her. "What?"

"I would have taken you more for a fun in the sun beach girl than winter storm type."

She pointed at her auburn hair. "I get this hair, my green eyes and fair skin from my Irish great-grandmother. I don't tan—I burn and freckle, in that order. I go to the beach armed with a ton of SPF 50 lotion," She turned toward the darkening skies, released a sigh. "But I love watching storms roll in—any kind of storm."

They stood in silence for a full minute, watched the clouds swirl, growing ominously dark and heavy with the promise of precipitation of some kind. The touch of his hand on hers, seeking, reaching out, had her facing him again. They stood there, gazes locked, his hand clutching hers. "What is this, Mack?"

"I'm not sure what it is now, but I have this sense of what it could be. There's something so…familiar…so easy about it."

Just for a moment she let herself hope. And then she remembered why she couldn't and stepped back, trying to pull her hand from his. "This can't happen."

He extended his arm, his gentle grip tightening, refusing to release her. "I know."

"It's only been a year since—"

"I know," he cut her off. "And I live four states away. I know. It doesn't make any sense at all."

She nodded, needed him to release her hand—willed him to hold on tightly. Nothing about this made sense. Seconds later, the wind changed, and she shivered from its chill. "That front's here and we'll get drenched if we stay put much longer."

He acknowledged with a nod.

A single, fat raindrop hit her face and Natalie freed her hand to wipe it away. She turned and walked away, his presence behind her a constant reminder of what couldn't—shouldn't happen.

\* \* \*

The temperature dropped a full forty degrees by 7:00 p.m., prompting Drew to light the fireplace. After an evening meal of Beth's savory home cooked soup and freshly baked bread, Natalie retreated upstairs. Mack had no desire to be alone and remained downstairs with his hosts, playing several friendly rounds of Crazy Eights and Spades.

Natalie ambled downstairs around 9:00, freshly showered, make-up free, wearing the plaid flannel pajamas she'd purchased during the mall shopping excursion, armed with a tablet type device. She grabbed an afghan off the leather couch and plopped herself down on one end. Duke appeared at her feet and rested his huge head on her thigh. Her fingers tunneling through the dog's thick coat triggered an immediate series of contented grunts and groans from the animal.

Irrationally envious of the dog, Mack watched until stomping from the front porch drew his attention to the door. The only other guests at the lodge entered the room, accompanied by a blast of icy air. The Coopers hurried inside, slammed the door behind them.

Beth met them at the door, offered to make each of them a cup of hot cocoa. They declined, saying they'd had a long day visiting nearby family, with more of the same planned for tomorrow, and headed upstairs.

Drew stood as well, stretched his back and groaned. "I'm about done for. Hauling that water in took a toll on this old back of mine." He looked at Mack and then Nat. "Can I trust one of you two to bank that fire if you're staying up?"

Mack waved him off. "I've got it, don't worry."

Drew's gaze fell on his dog. "You coming, Duke?"

Duke lifted his head lazily from Natalie's thigh, stared at his master for a second before returning to his position.

Drew chuckled. "Smartest dog we've ever owned—there's your proof."

Natalie smiled. "He's good where he is."

Drew dismissed his dog with a final wave and headed toward the back end of the first floor, the space filled with his grumbling. "I miss the good old days—when I could put in a day of hard work and not collapse from exhaustion."

Beth caught up to him. "Or wake up without my joints snap, crackle, popping like a bowl of cereal after adding milk."

Drew draped his arm across his wife's shoulders. "I could handle the sound effects if it didn't come with all the aches and pains."

Beth slipped one arm around her husband's waist. "Come on, old man. Let's pop a couple of anti-inflammatories and take our old bones off to bed."

"Good night, you two," Natalie called out.

Mack watched Nat as her gaze followed the older couple out of the room. He adored how one corner of her mouth lifted higher than the other with the slightest of smiles, and the sparkle in her green eyes, a direct reflection of that same smile. She turned away, her attentions shifted once more to the tablet and Duke.

Several awkward moments of silence later, she sighed. "Stop watching me. You're making me self-conscious."

"Sorry. I can't help but wonder." His comment garnered the desired effect—she faced him; her brow high with curiosity.

"Wonder what?"

He edged closer to her. "What forces of nature would have to occur to bring the two of us together." He shrugged. "A man can hope, can't he?"

She turned back to her e-reader. "I can't imagine what that would take." She plowed her fingers deeper into Duke's coat, and the old dog groaned his approval.

Mack closed the gap between himself and the opposite end of the couch, settled into the pliable leather cushions. "I always heard Golden Retrievers were highly intelligent creatures."

Natalie caressed the dog's large head. "He's a good old dog."

Another long pause of silence passed between them. "If the universe somehow threw a bone of a chance our direction, would you consider it?"

She adjusted her grip on the device. "Consider what?"

"Dating me."

Her eyes on her screen, she took her time answering. "That's a mighty big *if*, considering the four states of acreage between us, don't you think?"

"It is now, but you never know what wonders the universe can produce." He leaned forward, rested his elbows on his knees to get a better look at her face. "Would you?"

She turned her lips inward, kept her gaze on the screen. After several seconds she faced him. "I'm not sure it would be fair to you."

"Why do you say that?"

"Because, I won't know until I actually start dating again if I'm *ready* to move on—to put my husband behind me. What if I do and realize the timing isn't right? That first person would equate to nothing more than the rebound guy after a break-up in a serious relationship. I'd hate to . . ." She paused and took a deep breath, released it before continuing. "I think you deserve better than that."

"Why don't you let me worry about that?"

"No."

"No?" He straightened his back, not sure which of the two questions she'd answered so abruptly.

"You *do* deserve better than that." She lowered her feet to the floor and rose from the couch. "I don't want to discuss this again, Mack. Good night." She headed upstairs, Duke the dog hot on her trail.

Mack watched their retreat, again awed at Old Duke's intelligence. It took a full minute for her answer to finally sink in, bringing a smile to his face. Put there not so much by what she had said—but what she hadn't.

The only question now was whether to sit back and let the forces of nature blow their own winds in one direction, or initiate a little change in weather pattern of his own.

## Chapter 8

December 23rd

Natalie stretched, blinked several times and opened her eyes to the muted glow of morning light filtering out around the edges of her corner room's two windows. Shivering, despite the warm air pouring in from the central unit's overhead air vent, she got up and slipped her feet into her new slippers. Duke lifted his head from his spot on the rug and rose slowly, stretching his two front legs before him.

She approached the window, pulled aside the room darkening drapes, and gasped at the rarity of a snow-covered landscape. Soft, fat, snowflakes drifted down from gray skies heavy with cloud coverage. "It's snowing, Duke. Oh m'gosh!" She looked around for her robe, remembered she hadn't bought one on her recent shopping trip.

Bubbling with excitement, Natalie dressed in layers, both eager to get out in the fluffy white stuff, but aware of how cold it would be. She slipped into leather boots and her new coat before grabbing a pair of gloves and her hat, met Duke standing at the door. "Come on, boy—let's go play in the snow!"

She stepped into the hallway, looked up as Mack's door opened. "It's snowing, Mack! Isn't it fabulous?"

His face still lined with sleep, he dragged one hand through his ruffled hair, and yawned. "Mm, hmm— fabulous . . ." He slipped a flannel shirt over his white tee and buttoned it bottom to top.

She couldn't stop the laughter from bubbling up at the irony of his situation. "Poor Mack—you came all this way to get away from snow, and it followed you."

He stared down at her, his eyes hooded and sleepy. "You're a real riot, Nat."

"Don't worry. You won't have to shovel your way out of this snow. A foot is record breaking for us, and it'll melt on its own a day later at the first hint of sunshine. But I'm sure going to enjoy it while I can." She ran down the stairs after Duke, with Mack lagging behind.

She opened the front door of the lodge and stepped out, sucking in her breath at the icy air. Beth and Drew stood at the top of the stairs and faced her, their greetings of "Good morning!" cheerfully synchronized.

"There's Duke, the old traitor," Drew added, as the dog ambled to the edge of the wide porch and down the steps to do his morning business.

Natalie beamed at their hosts. "He kept me company all night. He's such a good boy."

"He usually sleeps in our bedroom when he's inside," Beth admitted. "I've never seen him take to a guest as quickly as he has to you."

Mack grabbed his coat from the rack at the door and pulled it on. "I've always heard animals are excellent judges of character."

Drew grinned as Duke headed back up the steps and sat at Mack's side, looking up at him. "I have, as well, and it seems he's taken a shine to both of you." He turned to his wife. "How do you like that, honey? Twelve years and we're pushed aside like a dirt bike in a store full of Harleys."

Beth leaned over to pet their dog. "I don't know. Should I be jealous, Duke? Have we been replaced?" The dog answered with a lick to the side of her face and wag of his fluffy tail. She laughed and straightened, wiping her face as Duke plopped himself heavily right on top of her and Drew's feet. "I guess that means he still loves us."

Anxious to play, Natalie headed down the porch steps into the yard. Her boots crunched on the snow, leaving a distinct trail of footprints in the fresh blanket of white. "It must have started snowing hours ago. It's so beautiful."

Mack followed her, adding his own footprints next to hers. "I came downstairs around 2:00 a.m. and it had already started accumulating on the ground."

She reached down, scooped up the damp stuff between her gloved hands. "You were still up at that time?"

"I couldn't sleep."

Natalie resisted asking why, and instead, packed the snow into a neat round ball before rolling it around on the ground. "Help me build a snowman, Mack. This may be my only chance for several years."

He scooped a handful of snow, frowned as he packed it into a tight ball. "You should be glad you don't see much of this stuff. This is what we call 'heart attack snow' back home."

"Are you serious?" She watched him discard the snowball to wipe both hands on his jeans.

"Absolutely." Mack reached into his coat pocket, pulled on the pair of gloves he'd purchased at the mall, flexing his fingers several times before reaching for the ball of snow again. "Imagine having to dig yourself out of six to ten feet of this stuff. It's so heavy because of the moisture in our area that people have heart attacks from the physical strain of shoveling."

"That gulf breeze brings in all kinds of humidity in the south. Snowfall is rare here, so we take what we can get. Shoot, I remember running the central AC during Christmas. My granny fussed one year because she'd been in the hospital with a broken hip during the only cool spell we had before Christmas. She'd been so upset because she missed out on what she calls her divinity-making weather—cool with low humidity."

"Divinity—that's the soft white candy, isn't it? I love it, haven't had any in years."

Natalie paused to glance over at the lodge. Beth and Drew had long since retreated to its warmth. She labored on her snowball for several minutes longer, looked up when Mack's next question broke her concentration.

"Is this big enough?" He stood next to an impressive sized snowball, at least two feet in diameter.

"How'd you get yours that big so quickly?"

"Don't look so surprised." He thumbed his chest proudly. "I got skills—I *am* a building contractor, you know."

"With decades of snow ball practice," she added, rolling her somewhat misshapen snow ball next to his.

"That, too." He lifted her snow ball and placed it atop of his. "Yours is the perfect shape and size for the torso. Now we need a smaller one for the head and we're in business."

"You work on that and I'll scavenge the area for accessories." She returned later with two sticks for arms and a hand full of dark rocks for the facial features.

Beth came outside, all bundled up and carrying a bag. "I thought y'all could use these."

Nat squealed in delight as she pulled a carrot, a long black and gold knitted scarf, and several black and gold Saints pins from the bag. She placed the carrot and scarf accordingly, used the pins as buttons on the torso, and took a step back. "Perfect!"

"Not quite," Drew called from the porch. "He needs one thing." He trudged across the yard, produced a black cap boasting a New Orleans Saints fleur de lis symbol on the bill, and a furry tuft of fake gold fur sprouting from the top. He placed it on the snowman's head and stepped back. "*Now* it's perfect."

They broke out in a muffled round of gloved applause. Beth produced a camera and got several shots of Nat and Mack together. Mack pulled up his phone's camera app and they gathered for a group selfie. Even Duke moseyed over and got in on a couple of shots.

Soon after, the older couple went back inside, claiming it was too cold.

Natalie stared at their creation. "I love our Saints snowman."

"He's okay. It'd be better with a Vikings helmet."

She gave him the stink eye. "Not around here."

His chuckle rumbled in the air. "You're from Mississippi. Why are you a Saints fan?"

"Biloxi's a hop, skip, and a jump from New Orleans. Most people in Mississippi are Saints fans."

"That takes care of the NFL—how about college football?"

She grinned. "SEC all the way, baby! But I'm an Ole Miss Alumni—class of 2009—so don't expect me to pull for LSU." She arched her brow. "That is, unless they're up against Bama's Crimson Tide. It's a given I'll pull for anyone *but* Bama. Old 'Big Al's' head is the only animal I'd ever care to see mounted and hung on a wall."

"I've never understood the correlation between the Crimson Tide and the elephant."

"There is none," Natalie said. "Story is they both came about from comments made by sports writers or announcers—nobody called them commentators back then. Crimson Tide has been around longer, something about the linemen being covered in red mud during a tight game between Bama and Auburn way back in 1907."

"And the elephant?"

"Sadly, that came about over two decades later during a game with Ole Miss. Bama went undefeated that year. Some guy in the stands yelled out *Hold your horses. Here come the elephants,* when the Bama team took the field. The sports writer put it in the article and the students ran with it."

"Why do you know so much about Bama when you're an Ole Miss graduate?"

"Know yourself and know your enemies—Sun Tzu's *The Art of War*— "

"He got that from an old proverb."

"I know." She sent him a sideways glance. "I guess you're a fan of the Big 10 division. Did you go to Minnesota State?"

He kicked at a mound of snow. "I joined the Army right out of high school, remember? Never could see myself sitting through four or five more years of schooling. But I've had season tickets in the past."

She scooped up a mound of snow and packed it into a tight ball. "Isn't their mascot a groundhog or something like that?"

He wiped his mouth on the back of his gloved hand. "A gopher."

She placed the ball on the ground and scooped up more snow. "Isn't it the same thing?"

His bark of laughter rang out over the silent, white landscape. "There's a difference, and they're the Golden Gophers for your information."

She offered an over-dramatic shiver. "Oooh, that sounds terrifying!" She placed the ball beside the first and scooped up another glove full.

He groaned and shook his head. "Go on—get it out of your system."

"Nah, I'll leave you alone." She grabbed all three of the snowballs and distanced herself before she turned on her heels and launched one that missed, whizzing past his shoulder. He looked up and got one right in the face.

He wiped the snow from his eyes and glared in her direction. "You did not just initiate a snowball fight with a Minnesota man." He saw the third one coming and raised his hand to swat it down. "Oh, baby girl, let me show you how it's done!"

She dropped to her knees, hurriedly made two balls, looked up to find he had three already in hand. "How'd you do that so fast?"

His chuckle sounded eerie in the frozen space between them. He didn't stop until he'd formed six snowballs. "Did I mention I pitched hardball all through high school?" He launched one that hit her squarely in the chest. "I started for the last three."

She launched one back at him, caught him on the back of his head when he spun to avoid it. "I didn't pitch, but I played first base in summer league as well as high school."

He answered with three in a row that had her spitting and sputtering snow. "You give?"

She pushed the wet hair from her face and launched another one that him on the arm. "Never!" When she took a step back, her foot went out from under her and she landed flat on her back.

* * *

He heard her screech before she hit the ground with a sickening thud. "Nat!" He rushed to her side, praying she hadn't hit the back of her head on anything hard. A friend of his once had a major concussion from a fall just like that. "Are you okay?" He stood over her. "Natalie!"

She lay there, her eyes closed, arms at her sides, still as death. Mack dropped to his knees, his chest tight with fear, leaned over her to check for any signs of injury.

Her hand came up quickly, smashed a snowball flat on the side of his face. He gasped as ice slithered inside the neck of his coat. She snickered, and her opposite hand came up with a second handful of snow. He blocked it, used his hands to hold both her arms down. "You play dirty."

Her mouth twisted in a grin. "When up against expertise like yours, all I have to counter with are my wit and womanly wiles." She tried in vain to move her arms.

"Yeah, well I was honestly afraid you'd hurt yourself. A fall like that can be dangerous—cause concussions." He leaned over, stared into her eyes.

She stilled. "What are you doing?"

"I'm checking for any sign of pupil dilation." He stared at her eyes for several seconds, inched his mouth closer to hers. What would she do if he kissed her now?

Her eyes widened. "I'm fine."

"I'd say you are." He inched even closer.

"Stop…let me up."

He couldn't have ignored the hint of pleading in her voice if he'd wanted to; his parents had raised him better. He released her arms, rose to his feet and reached for her.

She stared at his outstretched hand for a moment, as though weighing whether she should accept his assistance. In the end she took it, let him help her to her feet. Natalie brushed off her behind while he wiped the snow from her coat. "Sorry if I scared you. I'm sincere in my klutziness."

He brushed the last of the snow from her shoulder. "Lots of people fall in lo—I mean—snow. Lots of people fall in snow…you know…when they aren't accustomed to it. I mean, you don't even have the proper footwear for snow. Those leather soled boots are slippery in these conditions." He heard himself rambling, spun around and headed for the lodge as heat rose from his neck all the way up to his ears. What. The. Heck—was that?

He waited until he was nearly at the lodge's front steps to glance over his shoulder. She stood in the same spot, watching him. "If you stay out, be careful where you step."

"I will!" she called out.

He stomped up the front steps and pulled open the lodge door. Duke brushed past him to sit at the top step and bark at Natalie.

"Come on, Duke! Come play in the snow with me."

The dog stood, wagged his tail, then sat and emitted a strange combination of whines and barks.

Drew appeared at the door. "He's old, Natalie. This cold might have him feeling the aches and pains more than usual, kind of like Beth and me."

"Aw, I hadn't thought of that. I bet you're right." She trudged back to the porch and sat beside Duke, draping her arm around the dog's neck to pull him close for a hug.

Mack brushed past Drew, filled once more with a perverse envy for that dog.

## Chapter 9

The snow continued for most of that day, sometimes as lightly floating snowflakes, sometimes raining down in huge, heavy clumps of frozen precipitation. Both Nat and Beth spent most of the day on the front porch rockers drinking hot cocoa, bundled in coats, with electric blankets spread on their legs to keep them warm. Duke never left the spot next to Nat's feet, so she shared part of the blanket with him.

The Coopers, having left the lodge earlier that morning, called hours later to let the Brunson's know that their car had slid off the icy roads into a ditch. Mrs. Cooper's family members, local farmers in the area, had pulled them out with no trouble, no injuries, and no damage to the car. They'd managed to get the vehicle back to the family farm, but had insisted the couple remain where they were until driving conditions improved. Drew had been more than happy to refund the rest of their stay under the circumstances.

The local news showed video of dozens of the same situation throughout the area, while law enforcement at city, parish, and state levels plead with everyone to stay off the roads.

"No problem," Drew mused, after seeing the conditions. "I'm more than happy to spend the next few days holed up here in front of the fireplace. How about you?"

Mack rocked slowly in the chair inside the toasty warm room. "I'm in complete agreement." He stared out the window at the lengthening shadows, wondered how long Nat and Beth would stay out there on the porch. The temperature had steadily dropped with waning daylight, but the women had remained in place, determined to get their fill.

He thought of the dog at Nat's feet and faced Drew. "Is it truly unusual for Duke to get that attached to a guest?"

"Absolutely—Beth is concerned poor old Duke will have separation anxiety when Nat leaves to go home.

She says we may have to give him a dose of doggy Xanax." He sat back heavily in his chair. "Come to think of it, it *has* happened once before."

Mack stopped rocking, suddenly curious. "Who'd he get that close to before?"

"My wife." Drew faced him. "I told you we bought this cabin back from the couple who'd already turned it into a bed and breakfast, right?"

Mack nodded, sensing a twist to the story.

"Well, Duke was already here. This stray pup showed up a couple of years earlier and the Bennet's took him on as the Lodge's mascot, so to speak. When they decided to sell, they called us first, as previously agreed. I came out by myself to see what they'd done with the place—even saw Duke, but he didn't pay me any mind.

"I drove on home and talked it over with Beth. I don't mind telling you we were all over the board about buying it back—weighing the pros and cons of letting it go or keeping it as a B & B—couldn't make up our minds. The Bennett's hadn't done too well and were ready to take a loss to get rid of it."

Mack frowned. "Was it a matter of bad bookkeeping or some other reason?"

Drew leaned forward in his chair. "Well, neither of them could cook worth a flip and they refused to hire anyone. Who wants to stay at a bed and breakfast with lousy food? This is Louisiana—you can drive five minutes in any direction and dine at some place with good eats. We knew we could do better once word spread about Beth's good cooking. But did we want that kind of commitment?"

Mack stopped rocking and listened. "So, what locked you in?"

Drew's eyes glazed over as he spoke, as though he were reliving the moment. "We drove here together to discuss it with the Bennett's. I was leaning toward turning it down, but Beth was calm on the drive over, said not to worry. She told me she'd prayed the night before, and asked God to send her a sign if he wanted us to take the offer. I was skeptical, but she had faith that He'd let her know, one way or another.

Mack held his breath, waiting for the rest.

"As soon as we drove up, Duke ran out to meet us like he'd known us all his life. That dog walked right up to Beth and wouldn't leave her side the entire time we were here. The Bennett's claimed they were moving to a retirement home with a no pet policy and hoped the buyers would let Duke stay at the lodge. They figured he'd found his way to the lodge because he belonged here. By the time we left, Beth had made up her mind. She insisted Duke was her sign from God to buy."

Mack gave him a crooked grin. "That's an amazing story, Drew—if it's indeed true."

The old man slapped his thigh, his bellow of laughter filling the room. "Oh, it's true. You go out there and ask Beth about it, see what she has to say about your doubts. Go ahead. I dare you."

Mack caught sight of Natalie and Beth gathering their things to come back inside. "That's okay. I think the ladies are giving it up for the day."

"They lasted longer than I would have. It's too cold out there for these old bones of mine." He got up from the chair, groaning as he did. He took two steps then paused and faced him. "You know, Beth told me the other day she'd asked God to send her another sign when it was time to sell this place and move on."

He faced the door as Beth entered, followed by Natalie, the ever-present Duke at her side. "Maybe some of his signs are meant for more than one person at a time."

Mack considered Drew's statement throughout the evening meal of spicy delicious chili, served with crackers and homemade cornbread. Mack indulged himself with an extra bowl of leftover vegetable beef soup, as well. Rather than eat in the dining room, the four of them gathered around the television once more to watch the Vikings and Packers face off. In a show of solidarity, the others actually rooted for the Vikings.

Drew reached for his wife's hand after the final quarter and helped her off the couch. "Come on, love of my life, let's go to bed and get some rest for tomorrow."

Mack rose from the leather chair he'd occupied for the last three hours of game play. "What's going on tomorrow?"

Beth turned towards him; her eyes bright with excitement. "Why, it's Christmas Eve tomorrow, Mack. Have you forgotten?"

He actually had, without his mom around to remind him. "So it is. Do you have family coming in?"

"Well…" Beth glanced at her husband then turned a teary-eyed gaze on Mack. "Our kids were all supposed to arrive tomorrow afternoon, but driving conditions won't be any better tomorrow so we told them to hold off until it's safe. We'd rather see them a day or two late than put themselves and the little ones in danger." She blinked several times and turned away. "I need to check on something in the kitchen before I go up to bed, Drew."

"Sure thing, hon." Drew waited until Beth had left the room to speak to Mack and Natalie in a low undertone. "This white Christmas is pretty and all, but it sure throws a kink in the holiday travel plans." He faced Mack. "I know you must be thinking this is a whole lot of fuss over a little bit of snow and ice, but we're not prepared for this kind of weather. We don't have snow plows, snow tires, or chains on our tires to make driving in this mess less dangerous."

He paused, checked the kitchen door before he faced them again. "My wife puts on a brave face but I know she's disappointed. Christmas Eve night around here is kind of our thing with the kids and grands. Beth always goes all out for it."

Nat hugged herself and took a step closer to Drew. "Is there anything we can do?"

"Anything at all?" Mack added.

Drew smiled at them. "Just be here and get *involved*. Be a part of whatever we're doing. Trust me when I tell you this would be a heck of a lot worse if we were alone here. It's a blessing having you two around."

They nodded and headed upstairs, Duke hot on Natalie's trail. Mack paused at Natalie's door. "This stinks for them, doesn't it?"

She opened her door and walked inside to turn on a lamp. Duke followed her in, made himself at home by curling up on a rug next to the bed. "It does, and they're not alone, either. The evening news reported there are thousands of people stranded in airports and bus depots due to cancelled flights and delays."

He glanced inside her tidy room, everything in its place, her e-reader on the nightstand beside her bed. "Are you reading anything interesting?"

"A Christmas anthology—ten short Christmas themed stories by ten authors."

"I'm reading a police thriller right now." He'd tried to, anyway. Mack had found it difficult to concentrate on much since his arrival at the lodge, probably due to his timely introduction to Nat.

"I enjoy those, too, but I needed help getting into the Christmas spirit this year." She walked towards him, positioning the door a third of the way closed between them. "I guess I'll see you tomorrow. Good night, Mack."

He backed away from the doorway. "Good night." She closed her door and he went to his room, showered, and crawled into bed wearing flannel lounge pants and a T-shirt. He shivered under the cold sheets, wondered if Duke had stayed on the rug or if he'd jumped up on the bed with her.

He laughed at himself, wondering again how one man could find himself so envious of a darn old dog.

## Chapter 10

December 24th – Christmas Eve

Christmas Eve brought more of the same weather conditions as the day before. They woke to no running water due to a section of pipes freezing overnight. Several more inches of snow had fallen, filling all signs of tracks or footprints, creating a landscape every bit as white and pristine as the previous morning.

Natalie and Mack captured dozens of images on their phones. Clearly unimpressed by the white jacketed landscape, Mack retreated soon after to the warmth of the lodge. Nat stayed out a full hour longer, finishing up the snow wife for their existing snow man.

She finally pushed inside the back door of the lodge, red-faced from the icy air, her fingers numb despite gloves, and her toes numb inside two pairs of socks in her boots. Her damp auburn hair hung loosely around her face. She kicked off her wet boots and slipped into a pair of dry sneakers she'd left at the door.

Beth met her with a towel warm from the dryer. "Here, dry yourself off—that ice melts the instant it hits warm air. Just seeing you gives my old bones the chills." She pushed Natalie toward the fireplace where Mack stood with his back to the blaze, Duke lying beside him on the floor. "Even the dog's got enough sense to stay where it's warm."

She thanked her and smiled when Duke rose slowly to greet her, his fluffy tail fanning the air. Nat reached down to ruffle his fur. "Hey, boy—are you staying warm and dry?"

"Trying to, but some crazy southern girl keeps goading me into playing in all this stupid snow."

She straightened, grinned at Mack. "I know you're disappointed, but you know this is rare for us. Even though, I'll feel awful for Beth and Drew if their family can't make it in."

"I've got a feeling this will move on soon. Drew says crews have been working nonstop on de-icing the roadways and bridges for Christmas." He leaned closer; his voice low. "Meanwhile, he reminded me earlier to do what we can to distract Beth."

"That's fine with me, but we can't do it from here." Natalie took another minute to warm herself at the fire before heading into the kitchen with the ever-present Duke at her side. "Put us to work, Beth."

Mack clapped his hands behind her. "What can we do to help?"

Beth looked up from the turkey she rubbed with seasoning mix, her hands covered in clear disposable gloves. "I've got a ham in the oven for today, and I'll bake this bird tomorrow. I plan to whip up a couple of batches of divinity candy—my kiddos love it."

Mack licked his lips and beamed at her. "They're not the only ones so I hope you'll share."

Beth's eyes crinkled with laughter. "Of course, I will."

"How do you do it without water?"

Beth pointed to a couple of gallon bottles of water at the end of one counter. "Bottled water and these…" She reached for a box of disposable gloves. "These things are lifesavers when you can't wash your hands."

Natalie helped Beth in the kitchen while Mack assisted Drew with operation pipe thaw. She went to the faucet no less than a dozen times over the next hour, cringing each time it failed to produce water. "Aarrgh…" she groaned. "Cooking is such a *pain* with no running water." She reached for a gallon of water.

"I've experienced worse." Beth pulled off one pair of plastic gloves, deposited them in the trash before donning a fresh pair. "Okay, that does it for the divinity. It's time to make a batch of my gingerbread for a house and sugar cookies for decorating. I've been in touch with my children and they're all determined to make it here by tomorrow." She shook her head, blinking back tears. "We usually do this part together."

Natalie gave her a quick hug. "I'm sorry, Beth. It's too bad you don't have one of those hands-free video call devices. We could set it up in here so they could watch you bake."

Beth paused mid-step. "My youngest son is working overseas for Christmas and knew he wouldn't be in. He sent Drew and I something last week that has to do with video, but it's much bigger than a smart phone. We're technically challenged—figured we'd let the other two kids set it up. They all have one."

Natalie stared at Beth, her heart pounding in excitement. "Where is it?"

Beth entered her pantry and reached up onto a shelf. She pulled down a box and handed it to her.

Nat's eyes widened. "And you said they all have one of these?"

"I believe so."

Natalie emptied the box and set it up. Within the hour, she had Beth group video chatting with her offspring—one overseas, two in east Texas, a daughter-in-law in north Louisiana, and all six grandchildren.

By the time Mack and Drew walked inside after replacing a section of pipe that had frozen and burst, Beth was in the middle of whipping up a batch of sugar cookies with two of her granddaughters.

Natalie left the kitchen so the Brunson's could spend some screen time 'alone' with their family. She met Mack in the living room, sat on the opposite end of the couch from him.

Mack grinned at her. "You did a good thing, Nat. You saved their Christmas Eve."

"I don't know about saving Christmas, but that lady is definitely feeling better about the situation. I'm glad I could do something to repay their kindness."

"Drew still believes the roads and bridges will be passable early tomorrow morning."

"I hope so. Video chatting is better than nothing, but it can't replace hugs from your loved ones." Natalie bit her lower lip, deciding not to share the decision she'd reached when she woke early that morning. She had some major soul-searching to do and did that best in her own home. "I've decided to leave in the morning."

"But … aren't your parents in the Bahamas?"

"My girlfriend responsible for this trip is having a rough time back at her place. She was there for me when Craig passed—I want to help her through this."

He opened his mouth and closed it again. For an instant, she thought he'd ask her not to go. Instead he released a resigned sigh and gave one abrupt nod. "I understand. That's what a good friend would do, and—I bet you're the best."

She swallowed, forced herself to smile. "I'm no better a friend to her than she's been to me."

Mack got to his feet and paced in front of the fireplace. He rubbed his hands on his denim covered thighs then rested one hand on the mantle, adorned with another of Drew's beautifully hand-carved projects, a nativity scene he'd given Beth the previous Christmas. "Natalie, I know we haven't known each other that long, but . . ."

He spun around, faced her. "I dated Victoria a full year before I asked her to marry me. I spent the next year determined to fall deeper in love with her because everyone deserves to be with the one person who can complete them, don't they?"

Nat turned her lips inward, her mind reeling with thoughts she couldn't vocalize. *Please don't, Mack. I can't do this now. I'm not ready.*

"Back then I couldn't figure out how I could spend that much time with someone and feel as if I didn't know her." He adjusted his stance, flexed his fingers. "Now I'm wondering how I can feel as if I've known you all my life after only knowing you a few days." He looked up, took one deep breath and faced her again. "Couldn't we—"

She stood quickly, cutting him off with a wave of her hand. "No, Mack. No, we couldn't." She headed for the stairs, resolute in her decision. She'd spent last Christmas season miserable and crying over what could have been. She wouldn't do that again.

Time to look ahead at what could be—would be—if she could get her gears greased up and turning again.

* * *

Mack kept his gaze on her until she disappeared up the stairs, forced himself not to follow. He'd seen that look of determination before—the kind that conveyed a singular message. *This has to be done—so do it and be done.* He'd seen it when he looked in the mirror before he'd broken off his and Victoria's engagement. His heart had shown him he wasn't in it for the right reasons. He'd tried to love her the way she deserved, but had failed miserably. In the end, he'd had no other choice.

Vic had been justifiably angry at first, but had called a week later, admitted she'd known for the last few months. She understood his reasoning and eventually thanked him for having the courage to admit it and back away. He'd dodged that bullet and determined never to put himself or any other woman in that predicament again.

He walked slowly to the window overlooking the back yard. The snowman he and Nat had constructed stood as tall and solid as ever. Standing beside it, as though she belonged, was a second snow figure. Nat had draped a shawl over the torso, hung a small purse from one stick arm, and topped its head with a floppy hat. All the two of them needed was a snow baby to complete their snow family. He smiled at the thought and headed for the back door.

* * *

Mack sat on the couch later that evening, watching the local news with Drew. Viewers had sent in more than a dozen images and a couple of videos of the snowfall in the area. Some were of friendly neighborhood snowball fights, or snowmen, one snow castle, and several of vehicles sliding and spinning on roadways.

Drew chuckled from his easy chair. "I guess that seems silly to you, huh? All of this hoopla on the evening news over such a small amount of snow and ice."

Mack shook his head. "No way for people here to prepare for something like this. I'm not seeing reports of cars stranded in snow banks ten feet high, or people collapsing from shoveling, or trying to walk in blinding blizzards. Despite everything, this is still a break for me."

"It will have melted into a slushy mess by day after tomorrow. The roads will be safe to drive in the morning, and our kids and grands will be here bright and early." Drew grinned at him. "Enjoy your last night of peace and quiet."

Mack glanced first at the opposite end of the couch, suspiciously empty, then toward the stairs leading to the second floor. Nat had remained upstairs for the majority of the evening, coming down occasionally to utilize the washer and dryer. "Peace and quiet is overrated."

Drew filled the quiet space with bawdy laughter. "I'll remind you of that when our gang makes it in."

Mack stared at the blaze of crackling logs in the fireplace. This time tomorrow, Nat would be back in

Biloxi. And he'd be stuck at Mistletoe Lodge without her until his flight on January 2nd.

He took a deep breath, exhaled slowly before rising from the couch. "I'm going to head on up to bed. Good night, Drew."

"G'night, Mack. Sweet dreams."

Mack grunted, and trudged upstairs. He paused before Nat's door, his hand raised, tempted to knock. No light seeped out from under the door—he figured she must be asleep already, no doubt wanting an early start in the morning.

He turned away, entered his own room and shut the door behind him. He'd rise early, give himself one last chance to speak to her before she left. He showered quickly and went to bed, tossed and turned until the wee hours of the morning before falling into an exhausted sleep.

* * *

December 25, 4:30 a.m.

Natalie descended the stairs quietly, followed by Duke. She left her suitcase, one large bag, and her coat and purse at the door before heading into the kitchen.

She found Beth pouring herself a big cup of coffee, a tray of cinnamon rolls beside her, ready for the oven. "How early does someone have to rise to make it into this kitchen before you?"

Beth's delighted laughter rang out. "I've been up for an hour already. Too excited to sleep, I guess—Merry Christmas, Natalie."

Nat approached the woman and gave her a big hug. "Merry Christmas to you, too, Ms. Beth. And I hope you have a wonderful New Year, as well."

Beth returned the hug and stepped back; her left brow arched. "It will be. I feel change coming to Mistletoe Lodge, and to you also, dear." She winked and raised the mug of coffee. "Are you ready for a cup?"

Natalie sucked in her breath. "Can I get one to go?"

Beth frowned. "Where are you headed this early?"

"I'm going back to Biloxi. My friend needs me, and I have some things to think about. But I'll be in touch with you, I promise."

Tight-lipped, Beth pulled a to-go coffee cup from a sleeve in the cabinet. She filled it and set it before

Natalie. "There you go, Nat. I'm about to put these cinnamon rolls in the oven if you want to stick around for a couple."

Natalie stirred cream and sugar into her coffee and snapped the lid on. "It's tempting, but no. I want to get on the road—I don't know how many delays there'll be on the interstate."

Beth handed her a cardboard goodie box full of cookies and candies. "These are for your trip. I'll reimburse your friend's credit card for the early departure."

"Of course, I want the goodies, but the reimbursement isn't necessary."

"It most certainly is. You helped us spend Christmas Eve with our family. We are so grateful to you."

"I'm glad I could help."

Beth clasped her hands nervously. "Does Mack know you're leaving this morning?"

"I told him last night I'd be leaving this morning."

"Not this early, though …"

"No ma'am. Not this early."

Beth studied her for several moments before raising her hands in the air. "I guess you know what you're doing, dear. Be careful on the road, you hear? Have a safe trip."

Natalie smiled, gave her one last hug before heading for the door, shadowed by the dog. "Do you want me to let Duke out?"

Beth followed her to the door. "No, I'll hold his collar when you leave. Poor thing will probably try to follow you halfway to Biloxi and get lost."

Nat knelt and hugged the animal's neck. "I'll see you again, Duke. I promise." She grabbed her bags and headed out the door, trying hard not to look back.

After pulling out of the driveway, Nat paused on the side road to stare at the snow figures behind the lodge. She'd transformed the lone snow man into a couple by making a snow 'wife' for him the previous evening. Someone else had transformed the couple into a family by adding two smaller snow 'children', and what could only be construed as the family snow-dog, wearing a red bandana around its neck. Only Mack would have done something like that. She blinked several times and wiped a stray tear from her face.

Determined to stay focused, she removed her foot from the brake and drove off, sending one last glance at the snow family in her rearview mirror.

* * *

Mack opened his eyes to bright sunlight streaming through the curtains. He checked his watch, swung his legs out of the bed and stood. How had he slept until 7:30? He dressed quickly and approached the door, screeched to a halt when he saw a slip of folded paper with his name on it lying on the floor. He picked it up and opened it.

*Mack,*

*Don't be angry. I'm terrible at goodbyes, but so grateful we met.*

*If those forces of nature you talked about find a way— well, you just*

*never know what fate has in store for us. Merry Christmas!*

*XXOO Natalie*

His phone rang, and he reached for it, frantically hoping it would be Natalie calling. Ridiculous notion, since she didn't even have his number. The word MOM flashed across the screen. What should he tell her? *I met this lady, Mom. She's amazing and I'd love to get to know her better…even if it takes the rest of my life.* He pushed the button, brought the phone to his ear. "Merry Christmas, Mom. Is everything okay? It's two-thirty in the morning, there."

"Merry Christmas, son! I got up to go to the bathroom and realized you'd be waking up Christmas morning without me. It's beautiful, here, and I am having a blast, but I do miss you."

"I miss you too." For the next several minutes, she talked and he listened.

The line grew quiet suddenly. "Mack?"

"I'm here."

"What's wrong?"

"I met…" He paused, swallowed the confession. "I've met some wonderful people here, Mom. People who know you, and…it snowed, can you believe it?"

"Yes, I went to school with Beth and I heard all about the snow. Margaret's on one of the social media sites and she showed me videos and tons of pictures of the snowfall around there. My poor boy, you went down there to get away from it. Wasn't that a piece of rotten luck?"

He walked to his window and looked down on the snow family. "It wasn't so bad."

The instant his mom disconnected, he collapsed on his chair and stared out the window. He called the airline, tried to get an earlier flight out, with no luck. Flights at all major airports were backed up for days due to this weather and cancelled flights took priority. Mack headed downstairs, his heart heavy, aching with disappointment, and anxious for this day, this week, this entire year to end.

The Brunson's family members finally made it in, transforming the quiet lodge into a bustling hub of holiday activity. After meeting two of their children, three in-laws, and six grandchildren between the ages of four to nineteen, Mack decided the airline had done him a favor. The little ones were impressed with his and

Nat's snow family, and added several more members, accessorizing them accordingly.

The day ended with him feeling grateful to the Brunson's boisterous family for filling, at least partially, the void Natalie's abrupt departure had left in him.

* * *

December 26th

After a fitful night of sleep, Mack entered the kitchen late that morning, walking in during a serious discussion between the Brunson's and their two present children. He poured a cup of their strong coffee, grabbed a buttery croissant, and left the room immediately. He'd overheard enough of the conversation to know that someone had made an extremely generous offer on the lodge.

Mack finished off his croissant alone in the dining room and sipped his coffee. He stared out at the oak trees in the yard, the melting ice and snow on its branches falling like rain to the ground below. The local weather reports predicted temperatures to warm up to high-forties by noon, with an abundance of sunshine.

The south had experienced the rarity of a white Christmas, but its New Year's would be typically mild.

Drew appeared several minutes later with a carafe of coffee to freshen his cup and a plate filled with Mack's usual breakfast choice, bacon and eggs over easy. He placed the plate in front of Mack. "Mind if I sit?"

"Not at all, I'd like the company."

Drew settled himself and sent him a soul-searching look. "I guess you heard enough of the conversation to know we've got a buyer for the place."

Mack sipped his coffee and put down the mug. "Kinda difficult not to."

Drew chuckled. "Not like it's a secret or anything. Beth and I wanted to reaffirm that none of the kids had changed their minds and decided to keep it in the family. Looks like the place will have a new owner by New Year's Day."

"That quickly?"

"Yep—the offer was too generous to pass up." Drew sat back in his chair, rested his clasped hands on his belly. "I sense you're ready for a change, Mack. Am I reading you right?"

Mack let his fork drop to the plate, swiped one hand over his face. He struggled several seconds before coming up with the right answer. "I feel—I think—" He exhaled on an exhausted sigh. "The thought of going back to Minnesota permanently makes me crazy."

Drew grinned, gave his head a slow nod. "You're a southerner at heart, you know. It must be that fine Cajun blood flowing through your veins. The buyer is looking for someone to help run the place. Would you be interested in taking care of the day to day running of the lodge so the new owner can tend to the guests?"

"You mean a maintenance man?"

Drew cocked his head, his eyes squinted in thought. "I'm sensing more like an assistant. Heck, before it's all over with you could even be a co-owner or partner in this place if you're willing."

Mack scratched his chin, realized he hadn't shaved since Christmas Eve morning. Natalie's departure had really thrown him off balance. A line from her farewell note played over in his mind—*If those forces of nature you talked about find a way—well, you just never know what fate has in store for us.*

Biloxi was just shy of three hundred miles from the lodge. He knew this for a fact after checking it out on his phone's navigational system. He'd somehow talked himself out of renting a car—following her over there like a lovesick teenager. Three hundred miles was a darn sight better than fourteen hundred. Maybe this was fate giving him the slightest of edges. Hope expanded in his chest until a single thought formed, deflating it like the jab of a needle to a child's balloon.

*Mom needs me around. I'm all she has.*

Drew seemed to sense his dilemma, reached out to place a hand on his arm. "No pressure, son. Just think about your options." He got up from the table, rubbed the shoulder he'd been complaining about for the last two days. "Talk to your mom. You never know."

Mack finished his breakfast alone, went out on the front porch to call his mom, his stomach churning like a disturbed nest of bumblebees. She answered after several rings, her tone a mixture of sleepy and concern.

"What's wrong, son?"

He looked at his watch, consumed with regret. "I'm so sorry, Mom. I completely forgot about the five-hour time difference. It's only 4:00 a.m. there. I'll call back later."

"Oh no, you don't. You wouldn't have called unless it was important. Now what's bothering you?"

"Are you happy living in Minnesota, Mom?" Her silence had him wondering if they'd been disconnected. "Mom?"

"I'm still here."

"Tell me the truth. Are you?"

"Truth be told, I've been over those Minnesota winters for a long time now, son."

"But I've never heard you complain."

"You are my only child! I'm happy being wherever you are. I refuse to be one of those people who have to visit with their children on facetime or skype or whatever they call it. I want grandchildren someday, and I want to see them, hug them, and be physically *there* for them. It doesn't matter to me if it's in Alaska or Borneo. Now what's going on with you?"

"If I'm offered an opportunity to work and relocate here in Louisiana, what would you say to that?"

Her light-hearted laughter rang out over the phone. "Well, son—I'd say get those wheels moving in the right direction. I can name six couples who are ready and willing to buy my place. And didn't you say the lease on your condo was almost up?"

"It is," he admitted. "I'm a little surprised at your compliance to a move like this."

"I'm a southern girl at heart, Mack. Spending time with my cousin, hearing everything that's been happening with my family and friends back in Louisiana …" She paused. "I want to go home."

He dropped his head back on the porch rocker, eyes closed, and dizzy with a sudden rush of euphoria.

"Son?"

He swallowed several times, waited until he could speak without his voice cracking. "Mom . . ."

"Yes, Mack?"

"When you make it back to Minnesota, start packing up. You're coming home."

## Chapter 11

December 31st - New Year's Eve

Mack watched the two-man team setting up the fireworks display across the pond, more than ready for the evening's festivities to begin. Delighted with his decision to 'assist' the new owner, Drew had given him a phone number. He'd called, left a voice message saying he'd be willing to take care of the day to day maintenance of the lodge—for a competitive salary, of course. He had plenty of savings, and this would do until he found something more to his tastes, if that ever happened. He'd resigned his position with the construction company he worked for and cancelled his flight to Minnesota. He planned to fly back a week or two after New Year's, depending on how well he and his new employer meshed. Mack felt more at home with every day spent at Mistletoe Lodge.

He'd been in communication with the new buyers, one CMB, Inc., several times since then—first, through a series of back and forth text messages that graduated to emails with proper professional letterheads. After being offered a satisfactory employment package, he'd signed on with the corporation, agreeing to give them a minimum of six months.

Anxious to finally meet the face of CMB, Inc., Mack approached Drew as the older man kept watch over the driveway. "Are you that ready to be rid of this place, Drew?"

Drew faced him, jabbing a thumb over his right shoulder. "Beth and I are anxious to begin the maiden voyage in our new motor home tomorrow morning."

Mack looked beyond Drew at the forty-foot luxury vehicle parked on one side of the lodge. "Aren't you worried you'll get on each other's nerves in those tight quarters?"

Drew's gaze landed on his wife, who stood on the patio entertaining a group of guests. "Close quarters aren't a hardship with the right partner. You'll see what I'm talking about one day."

Mack's chest tightened—ached with loss as images of Nat materialized in his mind. He began and ended each day with prayers that this change would somehow bring them closer, both physically and emotionally.

"Besides," Drew interjected. "We've got plenty of room in that thing. I would've been satisfied with something half that size. I only need two things to be happy. One is a bathroom with a stand-up shower and a sit-down throne. The second is a soft bed that's big enough so I can sleep next to my wife." He winked at Mack. "But my queen deserves to live like royalty, so we bought a castle on wheels." He leaned forward. "It didn't hurt that we bought it from friends for a great price."

"It's a nice one, for sure. Any plans for if or when you two get tired of the nomad lifestyle?"

Drew nodded. "We'll sell it and move to one of those retirement homes for seniors with no upkeep. Something in Texas, closer to our grandkids."

Mack crossed his arms over his chest. "Sounds like a plan, buddy. Meanwhile, when can we expect the arrival of this corporate head of CMB?"

"Anytime now." Drew craned his neck to look behind Mack. "If I'm not mistaken, that's the new owner, right there."

Mack tracked Drew's gaze to a maroon late model Ford Explorer, watched as Duke shot off the porch like an excited pup and ran to the vehicle.

Drew's laughter rang out. "Yep, that's her, all right! Look at old Duke, sucking up—he already knows which side of his bread is buttered."

Mack stared at the darkened profile in the vehicle. *Her?* CMB, Inc. was a woman? Not that there was anything wrong with that, he just hadn't expected one way or another.

Drew pushed him toward the Explorer. "Well, go on. You're the one who'll be working with her—may as well get the introductions out of the way now."

Mack headed towards the parking lot, glancing back as the crazy old coot broke out into another round of chuckling. He shook his head and kept walking towards the vehicle. He rounded the front, saw a woman bending over Duke and ruffling the dog's furry neck. Obviously a dog lover, she cooed softly to the animal, speaking in low, soothing tones. The hood of her lightweight jacket had fallen forward, obscuring her head and face from him.

"Hello, I'm Mack Henry, and I believe we'll be working closely together here at Southern Lights Mistletoe Lodge."

She stood, pushed the hood back from her hair and faced him. "Hello again, Mack. I'm Natalie Bradford, the owner and operator of CMB, Incorporated."

Mack froze, too stunned to take another step. "Nat."

She laughed, clearly thrilled at his shock. "I can't believe Beth and Drew pulled it off. I asked them to keep it to themselves until I made it back down here."

He willed his feet to move, took several steps closer. "*You* bought this place?"

She closed the gap by another two steps. "CMB were my husband's initials—Craig Michael Bradford. He sold insurance for a living. I didn't know it at the time of his death but he'd purchased an accident policy that paid double and left me well provided for if anything happened to him. I can afford this place, along with several improvements I plan to make."

"I-I'm," Mack stammered. "I'm a little thrown off right now."

The cool wind blew Natalie's auburn hair into her face. She pushed it away with her left hand, the ring finger missing her wedding band. "I told you I was an Ole Miss Alumni—what you don't know is that I received my Masters in Hospitality Management with a minor in General Business." She jutted her chin toward the Lodge. "Compared to the hotels I've managed in Biloxi and Gulfport this will be a cinch—and a welcomed change. I've discovered over the years that I prefer the one-on-one with guests rather than the business end of it. This lodge will be the perfect blend of both for me."

He grabbed the back of his neck with one hand. "I don't know what to say."

"Say you're happy to see me."

He dropped his arm to his side and grinned. "That's a given."

She took another step toward him, shadowed closely by Duke. "Say you'll work with me. Say you'll take the time to get to know everything about me—and that you'll let me get to know you the same way." Natalie reached out for him with both hands.

He took her hands in his own, pulled her against him. "I can't believe you're here. I prayed for this."

Natalie stood on her tiptoes to give him the sweetest of kisses, pulled back and smiled. "I did too, Mack." She laid her face on his chest.

Mack wrapped his arms around her, holding on tightly, afraid to lose her again. "If this is a dream, I don't want to wake up."

She laughed; the sound muffled by his shirt. "It's no dream, Mack—only the forces of nature rearranging the fates to smile on us for a change."

He kissed the top of her head, rested his chin on it, and closed his eyes. "Thank God."

## Chapter 12

Christmas Eve – One year later

Natalie set her laptop on the coffee table in front of the sofa and adjusted the screen. Duke followed her and took his spot on the rug in front of the fireplace. "You ready to see Drew and Beth, Duke? I bet they miss you." She checked the time and called over her shoulder. "Mack, it's almost time!"

"Be there in a second!"

Natalie shifted on the sofa to make room for her husband of nine months. He came in carrying a tray with two steaming mugs of hot cocoa and a bowl of popcorn and placed it carefully beside her laptop. When the notification they'd been waiting for sounded Nat leaned forward and tapped the connect button on her screen. Within seconds, the smiling faces of Drew and Beth Brunson appeared before them.

"Merry Christmas!" the Brunsons called out.

"Merry Christmas to the both of you!" Nat said, blowing kisses from both hands. "Oh, you guys are adorable!"

Beth raised a hand to the Santa hat on her head. "You like it? The grandkids brought them for us. Drew said he felt silly wearing it, but I told him it'll build his character."

Drew flicked the white fuzzy pom on the end of his hat and grunted. "Used to be we could make fun of our grandchildren by making them wear silly costumes, but it seems they've turned the tables on us. Payback, I guess. How are you two doing over there?"

Mack leaned toward the screen. "We're great, Drew. The renovations to the top floor were finished two weeks ago and we've been at full capacity since then. The first-timers and the regulars from previous years all seem pleased with the changes to the rooms, although the two of you are missed."

Beth nodded. "That's great news about the renovations. Of course, we miss our guests too, but it sure is nice to be so close to our grands."

"I second that!" Drew chimed in. "Besides, you two are naturals. You'll become their favorites in no time."

"That little tree behind you is gorgeous!" Nat said, craning her neck to get a better look at it. "Is that your new apartment?"

Beth shifted over so Nat could get a better look at the tree in the background. "No, we're in a bedroom at our son's place in Texas. We decided to come here since they have more room. They put trees in each of the bedrooms just as we did at the lodge. It's become somewhat of a family tradition."

Drew looked at his watch. "The other two kids and their families should be here within the hour." He faced the screen again and leaned forward. "Now what's all the mystery with the envelope you sent us with instructions not to open until tonight? You know my wife can't stand this kind of suspense. Nosey Rosey's been driving me crazy about it since I brought it in from the mail yesterday morning."

Beth performed a dramatic eye-roll. "Oh please! You act like they didn't know you before today. These two know which one of us is short on patience." She shook her head and jabbed a thumb in his direction. "I finally had to hide the darn thing to keep him from poking at it." She pulled it out from her sweater pocket. "But I have it here so can we finally see what all the mystery is about?"

Mack and Nat exchanged synchronized grins and nods before facing the screen again. "Open it!" they chimed, in unison.

Mack slipped one arm around Nat's waist as she clutched at his free hand. "Here we go," he whispered to her as the older couple tore open the envelope. He pulled her closer as Beth held up the Christmas card and read it out loud.

She opened it and read the inside, along with the inscription that said to open the slip of paper, folded carefully and taped to the back of the card. She lifted the paper and gasped. "Oh, my heavens! Is this what I think it is?"

Drew squinted at the paper. "What am I looking at?"

"It's an image from an ultrasound," Beth said. "They're going to have a baby!" She raised the image closer to her face. "Wait, either I'm seeing double—" She looked up, her eyes wide. "Twins?"

"That's right," Natalie said, about to explode with pure happiness.

"Our babies are due first week of July," Mack added. "You two are the first we've told. We decided to tell our parents when they all come in tomorrow morning for Christmas dinner."

"We are so honored you told us first. Congratulations!" Drew said. "I wish you were in front of me so we could pass out the hugs."

"I'm so thrilled for you both," Beth added, holding the image to her chest. "You really haven't told anyone else?"

Mack pulled his wife closer, rejoicing in the closeness. "We wouldn't have met without you two or this place. It seemed fitting to let you guys know first."

"And we love you for that! This is the best Christmas news ever," Drew said, reaching for the picture in his wife's hands and staring at it again. "Twins—you two are gonna be busy for a while." He looked up suddenly. "You might want to start looking for some full-time help."

The Brunson's heads turned at the muffled sounds of children calling out. "Sounds like another part of our brood just made it in," Drew said.

Nat waved a hand at the screen. "You two go on and visit with your family. We'll talk later and please tell everyone we said hello and Merry Christmas!"

"We sure will—bye now!" Beth and Drew waved and ended the video call.

Natalie placed a hand on her belly. "It finally feels real now that we've told someone else."

Mack closed the laptop and moved it to the side table. "I know what you mean." He grabbed the mugs of cocoa and leaned back on the cushy couch, propping his sock covered feet on the sturdy coffee table before handing one mug to Nat. "I suppose Drew's right about finding some reliable help around here. Either for the lodge or to help with babies, one or the other."

Natalie sipped at the cocoa and snuggled closer to her husband, grunting in approval when he draped his left arm around her neck and shoulder. "I hadn't thought of it, but it's something to consider. I wonder if your mom would be interested in helping us out with the babies."

"Hmph, be careful what you wish for. Mom would move in with us if we'd let her. She's never forgiven me for making her wait so long for grandchildren."

"You think she would?"

"Forgive me?" Mack said, followed by a low chuckle. "Popping out two at a time just might get me there."

Nat reached for his hand draped over her arm. "Move in, silly. It would be so much more convenient if she were here with us. We could convert one of the remodeled suites upstairs for her to live. Put a kitchenette in it and everything."

Mack scratched his chin. "If we do that she may never leave."

"It would be wonderful to have her here. I adore your mom," Nat said.

"I do too, but I hadn't planned on living with her for the rest of my life."

Nat thought about it from his point of view, the wheels turning in her head. "How about if we construct a separate building with two complete apartments for both sets of grandparents? That way, she'll have her own space, and my folks will also have their space anytime they come to visit." She looked up at him. "We have plenty of land."

Mack nodded, mulling over her suggestion. "Kind of like a grandparent duplex—that sounds like the best of both worlds to me."

Natalie sat up and bit her bottom lip, her brow scrunched as though she were concentrating. She finally relaxed against her husband again and sighed. "We could be getting ahead of ourselves, though. Your mom may not be nearly as excited at the prospect of being a live-in babysitter as we are at having her here. I mean, she needs time to live her own life, as well."

"It's not as if the babies won't have two parents here on the property at all times. We could surely make it work." He squeezed her arm. "We have plenty of time to worry about finding help. Let's wait to see their reactions tomorrow."

## Chapter 13

Mack watched the three older adults at the table, waiting for what was sure to be some kind of explosive reactions. Nat's parents stared at the ultrasound images of babies A and B, then at each other, their expressions equal measures of delight and astonishment. His own mother's voice, wobbly with emotion finally cut through the silence.

"You wouldn't kid an old woman, would you, son? I am seeing two babies, am I not?"

Mack grinned at his astonished mother. "Not about something like this, mom."

"I can vouch for it, Ms. Marie. We're having twins." She faced her own parents. "Are y'all okay, or do we need to break out the nitroglycerin tablets?"

Her mom looked up at her, her cheeks shiny and wet with tears. "More than okay. We are delighted for you both." She turned to face Mack's mom. "And for the three of us as well, am I right Marie?"

"Goodness, yes!" Marie jumped up to give her daughter-in-law a hug, starting a chain reaction of hugging from everyone in the room. She finally dropped into her seat and sat back, dabbing her eyes with her napkin. "I can't believe this, kids. Not five minutes ago, Nan, Neil and I agreed not to bring up the subject at the dinner table and you go and spring this on us."

Natalie took her place at one end of the table and sipped her glass of tea. "What subject?"

"Grandchildren!" Neil said. "You have no idea how difficult it's been to keep your mom from asking how long it would take for you two to make us grandparents."

Mack sat on the end opposite his wife and eyed his own mother to his right. "Oh, I can imagine."

Marie gave her son a playful slap on the arm. "You've sure made me wait long enough, boy. Now, let's get down to specifics. When's the due date?"

"Around Independence Day," Mack said, sipping from his own glass of sweet tea.

Nan clapped her hands suddenly, and squealed. "Twins! I can't *wait* to tell the girls at book club!" She sobered and stared at him. "Are you planning to hire someone to run the Lodge? There's no way Natalie can keep working. Pregnancy with multiples can be risky; and she'll need major help afterwards, with *two* babies."

Natalie cut into the conversation with a dragged out, "Wee-lll, mom … Mack and I discussed this a little last night, and I guess it depends on whether or not any of you fit into the equation as to how we'll solve that problem."

Marie clasped her hands together. "If you're asking if we'd be willing to help, my answer is unequivocally *yes!*"

"Ours too!" Nan said, looking at her husband, who answered with his own nod of agreement.

"Just try to keep us away," Neil said. "I'm ready to sell the house in Biloxi and move closer. You're our only child and we want to be wherever our family is. On the way up here your mom and I admitted that drive was getting old."

Marie's eyes narrowed at Natalie as she rested her chin on her hand. "I know the two of you have come up with a plan, so let us in on it."

Nat took a deep breath and dove into the deep end of the potential babysitting pool. "How would you feel about us building the three of you a grandparent duplex next to the lodge? Either you can live somewhere else and come and go as you please or you could live there, full time and we'll pay all your expenses. The choice would be totally up to you but we see it as a win-win. You'd be helping us out, and it would keep all of you from spending any of your retirement income on housing expenses."

Marie slapped her hand on the table. "I love the idea, and I surely don't have a problem living on the property, as long as I have my own space. The last thing I want to do is become a nosy rosy mother-in-law."

Nan leaned closer to her husband. "I don't know about you, Neil, but I feel the same way."

Neil patted his wife's hand. "I do too, honey. We'll sell the house but we're keeping our camper. If we ever want to get away for a while, we'll just pack it up and hit the road for a week or two."

Natalie looked around the table, beaming. "I'm so relieved! Mack and I figure, between the five of us and any other sitters we hire to give the three of you a break when you need it, we could totally make this work. It'll be rough for a while, but of course, it won't be forever. Once the twins start pre-school it'll ease up some."

Nan smiled sweetly at her daughter. "Oh, by then, surely you'll have added another one to the fold."

"Or more," Neil added. "Given your penchant for popping them out two at a time."

Nat laughed at her child's over-zealous grandfather. "Rein it in, Pop. Let's get these two out of diapers first, will ya?"

Neil raised his wine glass into the air, his blue eyes sparkling with humor. "I'm just saying. I think I can speak for all three of us here when I say the more, the merrier."

Nan raised hers, clinking it to her husband's. "Here! Here!"

Her mom did the same, making it unanimous.

* * *

Natalie stood beside the blazing firepit later that evening, enjoying the crisp, cold air last night's cold front had pushed through. Her husband stood behind her, his arms circled protectively around her waist. She smiled when he leaned close, his breath warm as it carried the softly spoken words to her.

"I love you, Nat."

"I love you, Mack." She turned at the sound of her parents' laughter, saw they'd congregated on the back porch with her mother-in-law and a few other guests. Life was good. She laid her head against her husband's chest and gazed up at the cascade of sparkling stars against the velvety black canvas of night sky. Beth Brunson's Southern Lights. She released a long, satisfied sigh that earned her an extra tight squeeze from her husband, accompanied by a question.

"What's wrong?"

"Not one thing," she admitted. "I'm just amazed at everything that's gone right this year. Last year at this time, if anyone would have told me where I'd be today, I wouldn't have believed it." She felt the rumble of her husband's laughter against her back, knew what he would say before he spoke a single word.

"For I know the plans I have for you, declares the Lord. Plans to prosper you and not to harm you. Plans to give you hope and a future." He finished by placing his palms gently upon her abdomen.

Nat placed her hands atop his and burrowed even closer to his chest. That's exactly what God had provided—hope when she none—and a future.

And she would be forever thankful.

*The End*

I hope you enjoyed the first book in my *Southern Lights* series. Please consider leaving a constructive review on Goodreads or any book retailer website.

# About the Author

Lauren Gayle lives in a small town tucked away in southwest Louisiana with her best friend, her husband of 26 years. She  spends most days paying into her 401K at the J.O.B., hoping to avoid being a burden to her children in her old age. Most of her free time is spent pursuing her passion of writing, canning jams and jellies from various fruits harvested in her area, and cooking palatable delights or baking goodies for her hubby, co-workers, children and grandchildren. A voracious reader, she's hopelessly addicted to her e-reader as a means of getting to sleep at night.

Her first book, A Southern Lights Christmas, is the first in her four-book Southern Lights series and reached the status of **USA Today Bestseller** in October of 2019. She plans to release the others in the series by summer of 2021.

Lauren writes sweet, southern romance with a touch of humor and inspirational flair.

You can find Lauren (laurengayleauthor) on Facebook, MeWe and Parler or contact her via email at LaurenGayleAuthor@gmail.com.

www.ingramcontent.com/pod-product-compliance
Lightning Source LLC
Chambersburg PA
CBHW060846120626
46557CB00008B/938